This Book Belongs to

_____

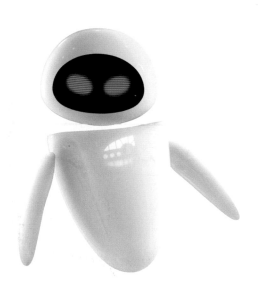

Disney Junior Encyclopedia of Animated Characters

Includes characters from your favorite Disney·PIXAR films

101 Dalmatians based on the book *The Hundred and One Dalmatians* by Dodie Smith, published by The Viking Press.

A Bug's Life copyright © 1998 Disney Enterprises, Inc./Pixar.

Cars copyright © 2006 Disney Enterprises, Inc./Pixar. Disney/Pixar elements © Disney/Pixar; not including underlying vehicles owned by third parties; Hudson Hornet is a trademark of Chrysler LLC; Fiat is a trademark of Fiat S.p.A.; Porsche is a trademark of Porsche; Mercury is a registered trademark of Ford Motor Company; Jeep® and the Jeep® grille design are registered trademarks of Chrysler LLC; Sarge's rank insignia design used with the approval of the U.S. Army; Chevrolet Impala is a trademark of General Motors; Mack is a registered trademark of Mack Trucks, Inc.; Plymouth Superbird is a trademark of Chrysler LLC; Cadillac Coup de Ville is a trademark of General Motors. Petty marks used by permission of Petty Marketing LLC; Volkswagen trademarks, design patents and copyrights are used with the approval of the owner, Volkswagen AG; Model T is a registered trademark of Ford Motor Company; Cadillac Range background inspired by the Cadillac Ranch by Ant Farm (Lord, Michels and Marquez) © 1974.

Enchanted is based on the screenplay written by Bill Kelly. Executive Producers Chris Chase, Sunil Perkash, Ezra Swerdlow. Produced by Barry Josephson and Barry Sonnenfeld. Directed by Kevin Lima.

Finding Nemo copyright © 2003 Disney Enterprises, Inc./Pixar.

The Great Mouse Detective is based on the Basil of Baker Street book series by Eve Titus and Paul Galdone.

The Incredibles copyright © 2004 Disney Enterprises, Inc./Pixar.

The Jungle Book is based on the Mowgli Stories in *The Jungle Book* and *The Second Jungle Book* by Rudyard Kipling.

Meet the Robinsons: RADIO FLYER is a registered trademark of Radio Flyer, Inc. and is used with permission.

Monsters, Inc. copyright © 2001 Disney Enterprises, Inc./Pixar.

Up copyright © 2008 Disney Enterprises, Inc./Pixar.

Ratatouille copyright © 2007 Disney Enterprises, Inc./Pixar.

The Rescuers, The Rescuers Down Under featuring characters from the Disney film suggested by the books by Margery Sharp, *The Rescuers* and *Miss Bianca*, published by Little, Brown and Company.

The Sword in the Stone based from the book by T.H. White.

Toy Story Copyright © 1995 Disney Enterprises, Inc. and *Toy Story 2* Copyright © 1999 Disney Enterprises, Inc./Pixar. Original *Toy Story* elements © Disney Enterprises, Inc. Etch A Sketch® © The Ohio Art Company. Slinky® Dog © Poof-Slinky, Inc.

WALL•E copyright © 2008 Disney Enterprises, Inc./Pixar.

Winnie the Pooh is based on the "Winnie the Pooh" works by A. A. Milne and E. H. Shepard.

Published by Disney Press, an imprint of Disney Book Group. No part of this book may be reproduced or transmitted in any form or by any means, electronic or mechanical, including photocopying, recording, or by any information storage and retrieval system, without written permission from the publisher. For information address Disney Press, 114 Fifth Avenue, New York, New York 10011-5690.

Printed in Malaysia

First Edition

1 3 5 7 9 10 8 6 4 2

Library of Congress Catalog Card Number on file.

ISBN: 978-1-4231-1670-7

For more Disney Press fun, visit www.disneybooks.com

Disney Junior Encyclopedia of Animated Characters

Includes characters from your favorite Disney·PIXAR films

By M. L. Dunham
and
Lara Bergen

Disney PRESS

New York

Why, hello!

Just follow me!

Dude!

Ih!

Haydee hi, haydee ho!

Oh, hi!

Uh, hi

Abu

First appearance:
Aladdin (1992)

Abu is the mischievous little monkey who is Aladdin's best pal . . . until Jasmine comes along. Did you know Abu never really speaks? He chatters and babbles so you can *sort of* understand what he's saying.

Abu Proves . . . Being Little Rocks!

Abu is so little that he is able to sneak fruit from a street vendor . . . and help keep Aladdin and some of his young friends from going hungry. When Jafar tries to destroy Aladdin by using Genie's magic lamp against him, Abu's small size enables him to get the lamp without Jafar's noticing.

Abu's Favorites

Favorite food: bananas
Favorite friend: Aladdin
Favorite place to hang out: Aladdin's shoulder

Abu knows his monkey business!

FUN FACT

The same actor who provided Abu's voice also made some strange animal noises for other Disney characters, including Joanna, the evil goanna lizard in *The Rescuers Down Under.*

ALADAR

First appearance: Dinosaur (2000)

When a huge dinosaur egg is dropped on Lemur Island, the little monkeylike lemurs aren't sure what to do—the egg is almost as big as they are! And they know the big baby is going to grow into a huge dinosaur. Still, the lemurs take the risk, and they end up with the kindest, gentlest iguanodon ever. His name is Aladar, and he even rescues his lemur family when a comet destroys their island. When they arrive on the shore of the Mainland, Aladar finds dinosaurs like himself—including a pretty girl dinosaur named Neera. Aladar eventually helps his lemur family (and Neera) find a home in a lush valley on the Mainland.

True love!

FUN FACTS

Aladar's favorite things:
- Spitting his little "sister" Suri out of his mouth, covered in dinosaur slobber
- neera
- Teasing Zini about his haircut

Aladdin

First appearance:
Aladdin (1992)

Just be yourself. That's exactly what Aladdin learns . . . even though it takes him a while to figure it out. At first, when Aladdin meets Jasmine on the street and saves her from being arrested, he doesn't know that she is the Sultan's daughter—or that she is running away from a bunch of suitors who all want to marry her. She just wants a simple life, while Aladdin dreams of what it would be like to live in a palace. Later, when he learns who Jasmine really is, he tries to impress her by pretending to be a prince. Oops—big mistake! Jasmine just wants Aladdin to be himself. It is only when Aladdin finally stops pretending, that Jasmine chooses him to be her husband.

Cool Quotes

- "We're outta here!"
- "Jasmine, I do love you, but I must stop pretending to be something I'm not."
- "Now, back to Agrabah! Let's go!"

Not-So-Cool Quotes

• "You're only in trouble if you get caught."

• "If Jasmine found out I was really some crummy street rat, she'd laugh at me."

• "The truth? Um . . . the, the . . . truth is . . . I, uh—I sometimes dress as a commoner, um, to escape the pressures of palace life."

Tricky Trivia

Q: When Jafar tries to enter the Cave of Wonders, he sends a thief named Gazeem to lead the way. Gazeem is told by the tiger spirit that he is forbidden to enter the cave. The tiger says that only one person, a "diamond in the rough," may enter the cave. Do you know who that is?

A: Aladdin

Q: Why does Jasmine need to choose a husband right away?

A: She is just a few days away from her sixteenth birthday, at which time, by law, she must be married.

Alice

First appearance:
Alice in Wonderland (1951)

Poor Alice! All she wants is to do something more fun than listen to her sister reading history books. But when she follows a White Rabbit (simply out of curiosity), she tumbles down a deep hole and ends up in Wonderland. Then she can't find her way home! During a series of magical mishaps, where she becomes quite huge and then quite tiny, she meets many interesting creatures, all of whom seem to enjoy mocking her, teasing her, or posing numerous riddles to her, which truly put her to the test. But when the Queen of Hearts threatens to lop off her head, Alice takes matters into her own hands, and escapes back home . . . where things seem much more comfortable and attractive than they had before.

To Alice, Wonderland is filled with riddles and nonsense, especially from the Cheshire Cat. Here's what he says when Alice asks him for directions:

Cheshire Cat: Oh, by the way, if you'd really like to know, he went that way.

Alice: [who has forgotten her initial question] Who did?

Cheshire Cat: The White Rabbit.

Alice: He did?

Cheshire Cat: He did what?

Alice: Went that way . . .

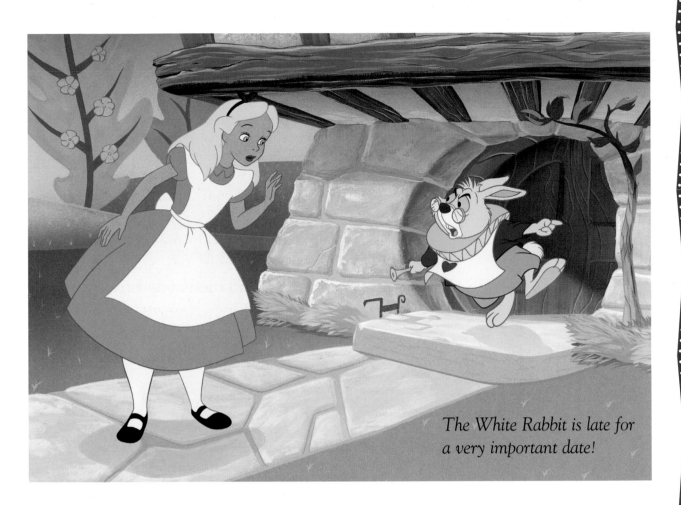

The White Rabbit is late for a very important date!

Cheshire Cat: Who did?

Alice: Uh, the White Rabbit.

Cheshire Cat: What rabbit?

Later, when Alice again asks for directions:

Cheshire Cat: "Well, some go this way, some go that way. But as for me, myself, personally . . . I prefer the shortcut." [*He pulls a lever, and a door opens in the tree below him.*]

Cool Quote

"I do wish I hadn't cried so much."

Did You Know. . . ?

When Alice plays croquet with the Queen of Hearts, they use flamingos as mallets and hedgehogs as balls.

13

Anastasia and Drizella

First appearance: Cinderella (1950)

Cinderella's two nasty stepsisters are just plain spoiled and mean. They make Cinderella wait on them all the time, and when Cinderella does get a chance to enjoy something, they do their best to ruin it for her. The reality is that these two are terribly jealous of the kind and beautiful Cinderella.

Stepsibling rivalry!

Tricky Trivia

Q: Do you know which sister is Anastasia and which is Drizella?

A: Anastasia has red hair and bangs. Drizella has brown hair with a part down the middle.

ANDY

First appearance: Disney • Pixar's
Toy Story (1995)

Woody and Buzz are both Andy's favorite toys.

To his toys, Andy is the best, most fun-loving boy in the world (or at least in his room, which is most of their world . . . except when they go on adventures, but that's another toy story). He treats them with respect, unlike his nasty toy-mutilating next-door neighbor, Sid, or the scheming toy-napper Al McWhiggin. Andy also has fun with his toys, playing endless games of make-believe. He is always ready to play. However, he never sees the true characters and personalities of his toys—they only come to life after he leaves his room!

TRICKY TRIVIA

Q: Can you name the puppy Andy gets for Christmas at the end of *Toy Story*?

A: Buster

Q: How do the toys get home from the airport at the end of *Toy Story 2*?

A: They drive the baggage-carrier truck from the airport.

Q: What pizza restaurant's trucks play a role in both *Toy Story* and *Toy Story 2*?

A: Pizza Planet

15

Ariel

First appearance:
The Little Mermaid (1989)

Ariel, the Little Mermaid, longs for adventure and romance . . . and to visit the human world. But her father, King Triton, thinks human beings are terribly dangerous to merpeople, so he forbids her any contact with them. Still, the mischievous princess of the undersea world risks everything—not just her beautiful mermaid voice, but also (unbeknownst to her) her father's reign over the undersea kingdom— in order to have three days on land as a human. All she wants is to meet Prince Eric, the love of her life. Luckily, both sea creatures and humans come to her rescue, and she herself pulls off some heroic feats in order to save the undersea world from the wicked sea witch, Ursula. She also wins the heart of Prince Eric and convinces her father to allow her to stay on land as a human so that she can be the prince's wife.

Did you know. . . ?

Ariel is given three days to receive a kiss of true love from Eric. If she succeeds, she will be able to remain a human, but if she fails, she will become a slave to the wicked Ursula.

Ariel tests out her brand-new toes.

Tricky Trivia

Q: Do you know how old Ariel is in *The Little Mermaid*?

A: Sixteen

Q: Why doesn't Eric immediately fall in love with Ariel?

A: Eric fell in love with the girl who rescued him, and all he remembers about her is her beautiful singing voice. But Ariel traded her voice in exchange for becoming human, so Eric doesn't realize that she is the same girl.

Q: Who is Ariel's best friend?

A: Flounder

FUN FACT

When Ariel first becomes a human, she has no clothes to wear. Luckily, she finds an old piece of sail to wrap around herself!

Will Eric kiss Ariel and break the spell?

Atta

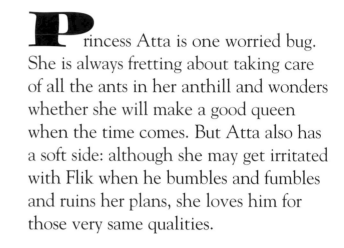

First appearance:
Disney • Pixar's A Bug's Life (1998)

Princess Atta is one worried bug. She is always fretting about taking care of all the ants in her anthill and wonders whether she will make a good queen when the time comes. But Atta also has a soft side: although she may get irritated with Flik when he bumbles and fumbles and ruins her plans, she loves him for those very same qualities.

Atta Girl!

Though she is in intense training to take over as queen of the anthill, Atta always pulls through when trouble strikes: "Now, it's going to take everyone's involvement to make this plan a reality. I know it's not our tradition to do things differently. But if our ancestors were able to build this anthill, we can certainly rally together to build this bird."

FUN FACTS

- Princess Dot is second in line to become queen after Atta.
- The Queen's throne is a folded leaf.
- When Atta becomes queen, her crown is a flower.

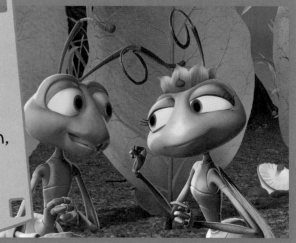

Flik and Atta are all tangled up!

Aunt Sarah, Si, and Am

First appearance:
Lady and the Tramp (1955)

As is true with many truly mean villains, Aunt Sarah and her two cats, Si and Am, are very sneaky. Aunt Sarah seems perfectly nice when Jim Dear and Darling are around, but when they leave, she treats Lady terribly. And her two cats are even worse. As soon as there are no humans around, they begin to ruin Jim Dear and Darling's living room—they even threaten the goldfish! When Lady tries to rescue the fish and keep some order in the living room, the cats screech for help, and Aunt Sarah comes running. That's when Aunt Sarah takes Lady to get fitted for a muzzle. Luckily, Tramp comes along and helps free Lady. Then, Jim Dear and Darling return just in time to rescue Lady and her new friend, Tramp, before Tramp gets put in the pound by Aunt Sarah. Hopefully, Aunt Sarah and her nasty cats will never be invited to visit again!

They're two crazy cats!

Aurora

First appearance: Sleeping Beauty (1959)

At her birth, Princess Aurora receives three good wishes and one terrible curse. The good fairies give her the gift of song, beauty . . . and a way to reverse Maleficent's curse (that the girl will prick her finger on a spinning wheel and die before her sixteenth birthday). Still, Maleficent's words are frightening to all who love the tiny princess. As a result, the three good fairies take Aurora deep into the woods, where they raise her in secrecy. She lives happily as a peasant girl and has no idea that she is a princess. Then, on the day of her sixteenth birthday, she returns to the castle, pricks her finger, and falls into a deep sleep. Luckily, her one true love, Prince Phillip (who has been imprisoned by Maleficent), battles the evil fairy and finally frees himself to go to Aurora and give her True Love's Kiss. She awakens to a life of love and happiness as a true princess.

Love at first sight

Tricky Trivia

Q: What are the names of the three good fairies who raise Aurora?

A: Flora, Fauna, and Merryweather

Q: What name is Aurora given by the fairies when she is taken away from the palace to grow up in the woods?

A: Briar Rose

Bagheera

First appearance: The Jungle Book (1967)

Serious and always looking out for Mowgli's safety, Bagheera has a tough time keeping his friend Baloo the bear in line. But Bagheera only tries to stop the fun and games because he worries about Mowgli. Now, here's the real secret: Bagheera actually likes Baloo, too—he just finds him really, really frustrating.

Bagheera goes on a wild ride!

Did You Know...?

• Bagheera is the narrator of *The Jungle Book*.
• Bagheera rescues baby Mowgli, and insists several years later that Mowgli leave his jungle family and go to live in the Man-village, where he can be safe from the villainous tiger, Shere Khan.
• When Bagheera thinks Baloo has been killed by Shere Khan, he gives a moving speech about his friend. Baloo awakens during the speech but pretends to be unconscious so he can hear Bagheera's praise.

Baloo

First appearance: The Jungle Book (1967)

Mowgli accidentally meets this big ol' gray bear when the Man-cub is trying to avoid being sent to the Man-village to live. Mowgli wants to stay in the jungle with his animal friends, rather than go live in a village with other humans, and the relaxed and fun-loving Baloo is willing to help. Baloo teaches Mowgli how to be a bear, and Mowgli just adores him. But when Shere Khan threatens Mowgli's life, Baloo becomes serious and fights the vicious tiger—the bear will do anything to save his "Little Britches."

Tricky Trivia

Q: Do you know what Mowgli calls Baloo?

A: "Papa Bear"

Q: The actor Phil Harris did Baloo's voice. What other voices did he play?

A: Little John in *Robin Hood* and O'Malley in *The Aristocats*

Boy and bear— best buddies!

FUN FACTS

Baloo's favorite things:
- Scratching his back against trees
- Eating (bananas, honey, ants, and anything else he can digest)
- Floating downriver on his back
- Being lazy
- Mowgli

22

Bambi

First appearance: Bambi (1942)

When Bambi the fawn is born, the forest comes alive with excitement. "The young prince is born!" rabbits and skunks and birds cry as they head to the place where he is resting with his mother. Bambi is, indeed, a prince. His father, a noble buck, is the Great Prince of the Forest. Bambi's bond with his mother, however, is what helps shape his character and integrity. She, along with his father, teaches him all about the forest, the seasons, how to get food, and how to follow in his father's footsteps as leader of the woodlands.

The young prince makes some new friends.

Tricky Trivia

Q: What is the name of the deer who is Bambi's rival for Faline's love?

A: Ronno

FUN FACT

Real deer were brought to the Disney studios so that the *Bambi* animators could study how they moved, in order to draw them better.

23

Basil of Baker Street

First appearance:
The Great Mouse Detective *(1986)*

Even though he seems an awful lot like the great detective Sherlock Holmes, Basil is really a tiny mouse. Brilliant and determined to help little Olivia Flaversham find her father, Basil also wants to beat his rival, the evil Professor Ratigan. Impressed with his own cleverness, Basil goes about his business with the bumbling and lovable Dr. Dawson by his side. And in the end, Basil triumphs—not only by rescuing Olivia and her father but also by beating mean old Ratigan once and for all.

FUN FACTS

- Some people believe Basil was named for the actor Basil Rathbone, who played Sherlock Holmes in many live-action films.
- Basil's address is 221½ Baker Street (the basement section).

Basil, hard at work in his laboratory

The Beast

First appearance:
Beauty and the Beast *(1991)*

*O*nce a vain young prince, the Beast cruelly turned away a peddler woman on a snowy night. Big mistake! The woman was an enchantress, and as punishment she not only transformed him into a Beast but also turned all his servants into enchanted household objects.

Belle and her Beast

Now the Beast has to learn to love and be loved before the last petal falls from a magical rose. If he does, he will become human again, along with his servants. The Beast is convinced no one could ever love him. But in the end, he not only learns to show his kindness, but he also proves his courage. Then he earns Belle's love . . . and becomes human again.

FUN FACTS

• The Beast has a bear's body, a lion's mane, a buffalo's head, a boar's tusks, and a wolf's tail and legs!
• The Beast actually becomes human just *after* the last petal falls from the magical rose.

Belle

First appearance:
Beauty and the Beast *(1991)*

Belle loves books for lots of reasons —but mostly because they take her on imaginary adventures where she can visit faraway lands and dream of excitement and romance.

When Belle meets the Beast, she thinks he is horrible and cruel for imprisoning her father. Courageously, she manages to convince the Beast to let her trade places with her father and stay at the Beast's castle. There, she finds a kind soul beneath the Beast's gruff exterior, and she literally brings life back to a once happy castle by falling in love with him.

Cool Quotes

Declining arrogant Gaston's offer of marriage: "I'm sorry, Gaston. . . . I just don't deserve you."

When Belle refuses to leave her room to join the Beast for dinner, he roars at her: "You can't stay in there forever!" To which she replies: "Yes, I can!"

Bookworm Belle

Bernard

First appearance: The Rescuers *(1977)*

This bumbling but lovable mouse transforms from helper to hero in the eyes of the all-mouse Rescue Aid Society. The R.A.S. is made up entirely of an elite group of mice from around the world. Bernard is the R.A.S. handy-mouse until Miss Bianca chooses him to be her companion for the very important rescue of Penny. Though much less adventurous than the glamorous Miss Bianca, Bernard nevertheless takes his assignment very seriously: what could be more important than rescuing a little orphan girl? In the process, Bernard wins Bianca's heart—simply by allowing her to see the grandness of his own.

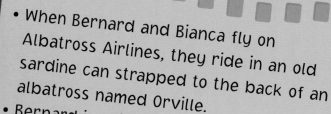

Fireworks go off whenever Bernard and Bianca get together!

FUN FACTS

- When Bernard and Bianca fly on Albatross Airlines, they ride in an old sardine can strapped to the back of an albatross named Orville.
- Bernard is voiced by funnyman Bob Newhart.

Bianca

First appearance: The Rescuers (1977)

Bianca is by far the most glamorous member of the R.A.S. (Rescue Aid Society) . . . and probably its best singer, too. A mouse (like all the other R.A.S. members), she is the official delegate from Hungary. Though she has her pick of any R.A.S. member to go with her on her mission to rescue the orphan Penny, she chooses Bernard. The reason? Bernard had shown remarkable (though somewhat clumsy) ability when he tumbled into a bottle, retrieved Penny's message for help, and struggled back out. (And though no one knows for certain, we think she may already have developed a bit of a crush on him as well.)

Evinrude takes Bianca and Bernard on a wild ride!

FUN FACTS

- Bianca is very brave.
- Nearly every member of the almost all-male R.A.S. has a crush on Miss Bianca.
- Miss Bianca prefers to wear only the latest fashions.
- The actress Eva Gabor provided the voice for Bianca.

Cool Quote
"Penny, dear, don't cry. We're here to help you."

The Blue Fairy

First appearance: Pinocchio *(1940)*

Though she does not appear very often in the film *Pinocchio*, the Blue Fairy does make all the difference in the world for the little puppet. First of all, she assigns Jiminy Cricket as Pinocchio's conscience. Although the little cricket has a hard time keeping Pinocchio out of trouble, he does stay true to him and does do his best to keep him on the straight and narrow. The Blue Fairy also can tell when Pinocchio is lying. His nose grows into a rather long tree branch as he fibs! Finally, it is the Blue Fairy who, at the end of the film, deems Pinocchio to be good—good enough, in fact, for her to turn him from a puppet into a real boy.

Cool Quotes

"Little puppet made of pine, wake! The gift of life is thine!"

"You may be a real boy someday, but first you must prove yourself brave, truthful, and unselfish. You must learn to choose between right and wrong."

The Blue Fairy brings Pinocchio to life.

Bolt

First appearance: Bolt (2008)

Bolt and his biggest fan

It's not Bolt's fault that he thinks he's a superdog. After all, he's spent almost his whole life on the set of a hit TV show. So after the network films an episode in which his person, Penny, is kidnapped, Bolt believes that she's really been captured. He sets out to rescue her and, though he doesn't know it, lands in the real world.

Bolt soon finds himself on a cross-country adventure, along with two companions—Rhino, the TV-loving hamster who worships the ground Bolt walks on, and Mittens, the jaded alley cat who breaks the news to Bolt that his "superpowers" aren't, in fact, real. Still, Bolt proves in the end that even an ordinary dog can be a hero.

Tricky Trivia

Q: Who are the enemies Bolt is determined to defeat?

A: Dr. Calico and the Green-Eyed Man

Q: What are some of Bolt's TV superpowers?

A: Heat vision, super strength, and a supersonic bark

Q: What is the one material that Bolt believes weakens his powers?

A: Packing peanuts

Boo

First appearance: Disney·Pixar's Monsters, Inc. (2001)

Boo first pops up in Sulley's life when she accidentally gets through her closet door and ends up on the Monsters, Inc. Scare Floor. The big, scary monster is terrified of her. She is a child and is therefore (in Sulley's mind) highly toxic. Not knowing what else to do, Sulley tries to hide her and then send her home. In the process, this innocent child terrifies many a monster in Monstropolis. Boo's endearing personality, however, eventually wins the heart of Sulley, then that of his best friend, Mike—so much so that the two are willing to risk everything in order to save her and return her safely home.

Boo and "Kitty," aka Sulley

FUN FACTS

- The film's creators considered making Boo a little boy at first.
- Even though Boo can hardly get an understandable word out of her mouth, she is able to pronounce "Mike Wazowski" almost perfectly.

BULLSEYE

First appearance: Disney • Pixar's Toy Story 2 (1999)

Woody's trusty steed from the *Woody's Roundup* TV show turns out to be just as loyal in real life as he is on TV. Whether he's licking Woody on the face like a pet dog or galloping under an airplane to catch Woody before he falls to the ground, Bullseye is always right on target.

Did You Know . . . ?

Bullseye doesn't speak. Unlike the other toys, who talk as soon as humans leave the room, Bullseye is more like a pet. He comes to life, but doesn't speak to his friends.

CHARACTER TRAITS

• Faithful
• Loyal
• Puppylike

The gang's (almost) all here!

BUZZ LIGHTYEAR

*First appearance: Disney • Pixar's
Toy Story (1995)*

When Andy gets the one toy he really wants for his birthday—Buzz Lightyear—it sends the rest of the toys in Andy's room into a panic. They are all worried that they will be thrown away or forgotten when this newer, shinier toy enters their little world. But Buzz Lightyear is most threatening to Woody, who has been Andy's favorite toy until now. Eventually, though, the rivalry between Woody and Buzz turns into a true friendship. Now the toys are friends for life!

COOLEST QUOTE

"To infinity . . . and beyond!"

TRICKY TRIVIA

Q: What's the difference between Buzz Lightyear and the newer Buzz model he meets at Al's Toy Barn?

A: The newer Buzz has a utility belt.

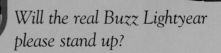

Will the real Buzz Lightyear please stand up?

33

Captain Hook

First appearance: Peter Pan (1953)

"**S**meeeeee!" Captain Hook, though a villainous pirate, is really quite cowardly, often calling for help from his clumsy first mate. Hook's number-one goal is revenge on Peter Pan, who once cut off the pirate's left hand and fed it to a crocodile. Hook is determined to find the Lost Boys' hideout, and he is always coming up with schemes to trap Peter—like kidnapping Tiger Lily. Unfortunately for the old "codfish," his devious plans are never successful because he is constantly outwitted by his archrival, Peter Pan. And Peter always manages to embarrass Hook in the process.

Captain Hook and Smee in Never Land

Tricky Trivia

Q: How does Hook know when the crocodile is nearby?

A: He hears a ticking noise. (The crocodile makes a ticking noise because it swallowed a clock!)

Q: Can you name seven of Hook's pirates?

A: Black Murphy, Skylights, Bill Jukes, Turk, Mullins, Starkey, and Smee

Cheshire Cat

First appearance:
Alice in Wonderland *(1951)*

This cat is most often remembered for his wide, full grin, which usually appears before the rest of his body is visible. But when his body does appear, it is also quite remarkable—covered as it is with pink stripes. The Cheshire Cat seems to enjoy teasing Alice with this partial appearing and disappearing act. He also confuses her with riddles, first sending her to meet the Mad Hatter and then the Queen of Hearts. The Mad Hatter is of no help at all, but the meeting with the Queen of Hearts, as bizarre and crazy as it is, ends up leading Alice home, after all. So, despite his mischievous nature, the Cheshire Cat does help Alice get home—in a very roundabout way.

The cat and the Queen

Character Traits
- Mischievous
- Bemusing
- Mysterious
- Evasive

Cool Quote
"All ways here, you see, are the Queen's ways."

Chicken Little

First appearance: Chicken Little (2005)

Chicken Little and his friends find an alien.

Chicken Little is small for his age, but he's got a big imagination and an even bigger heart. Mostly, Chicken Little wants to make his dad, the famous sports star Buck Cluck, proud. But it's not easy when the whole town thinks he's crazy for once believing that the sky was falling when an acorn hit him on the head.

Despite "the unfortunate acorn incident" from his past, Chicken Little is determined to redeem his reputation in Oakey Oaks. With the help of his faithful friends—and his father—he actually ends up saving the world from alien invaders! (And returning a lost alien child to its very worried parents.)

Tricky Trivia

Q: What brought the aliens to Earth in the first place?

A: Acorns!

Q: What are Chicken Little's best friends' names?

A: Abby Mallard, Runt of the Litter, and Fish Out of Water

Q: What sport did Chicken Little's dad play?

A: Baseball

Cool Quotes

"The sky is falling! Run for your lives!"

"Come on, Dad. We've got a planet to save!"

"I am the champion!"

Chip and Dale

First appearance: Private Pluto (1943)

Chip and Dale are two little chipmunks with two great big personalities. Chip is more responsible and no-nonsense, while Dale is a bit more scatter-brained and easygoing. They are always trying to gather a great stock-pile of acorns and other food . . . and if in the process they can tease their friends, like Donald Duck and Pluto, all the better!

The chipmunks also show up as a crime-fighting team in *Chip 'n' Dale Rescue Rangers.* There, they use their combined detective skills and clever gadgets to aid anyone in need of help.

The chipmunks gather acorns.

Did You Know . . . ?

It's easy to tell the chipmunks apart:
• Chip has a small black nose and one buck tooth.
• Dale has a big red nose and two gap teeth.

Cinderella

First appearance: Cinderella (1950)

Cinderella awakens every day to a simple life of servitude . . . in her very own home. Her stepmother (Lady Tremaine), her stepsisters (Anastasia and Drizella), and even their cat, Lucifer, constantly require her to wash and clean, sweep and mop, cook and serve. But Cinderella always has a lovely attitude and enjoys the company of her animal friends—the birds that awaken her and help her get dressed each morning, Bruno the dog, Major the horse, and most of all, the mice. But one magical night, all that changes for Cinderella when her Fairy Godmother helps her attend the Prince's royal ball. Cinderella and the Prince fall in love. All too soon, however, the magical night is over. The clock strikes midnight, and Cinderella runs out of the castle, accidentally leaving her glass slipper behind as she returns to her life of servitude. But then

Cinderella wants to go to the ball with her stepsisters.

the King sends the Grand Duke out to find the maiden whose foot fits into the glass slipper. Lady Tremaine, realizing it is none other than Cinderella, locks her in the attic. This is when the mice, including Gus and Jaq, prove not only to be her friends but also her champions. They bravely sneak past Lady Tremaine and Lucifer in order to take the key to Cinderella. Then she is able to escape her attic room in time to meet the Grand Duke and show him that she has the glass slipper that matches the one she left behind on the palace steps. Cinderella is soon reunited with the Prince, and they get married and live happily ever after.

FUN FACTS

- Cinderella loses her *left* slipper as she races down the palace steps at midnight.
- The Prince's real name is Charming—he's Prince Charming.
- When Cinderella dances—and falls in love—with Prince Charming, she doesn't even realize he's the Prince!

Clank, Bobble, and Fairy Mary

First appearance: Tinker Bell (2008)

Clank, Bobble, and Fairy Mary are Tinker Bell's fellow tinker fairies, and they show her the ropes when she first arrives in Pixie Hollow. In fact, easygoing Clank and Bobble even cover for Tink when she puts off tinkering and decides to give various nature talents a try. But Fairy Mary—a stickler for details—has little patience for Tink's wandering. As one who adores her workshop, she simply can't imagine how Tink could care about anything but tinkering.

Did You Know . . . ?

The tinker fairies have a work song. It goes:
Fiddle and fix, craft and create,
Carve acorn buckets to hold flower paint;
Preparing for spring, we do all this and more.
Yes, being a tinker is never a bore!

Clank and Bobble are thrilled that Tink is a tinker fairy!

Cool Quotes

"You can't change who you are, nor should you want to."
–Fairy Mary

"We're pleased as a pile of perfectly polished pots you're here!" –Bobble

"Spring won't spring itself!"
–Clank

Fairy Mary is happy to have another pair of hands.

Tricky Trivia

Q: What is Bobble's full name?

A: Phineas T. Kettletree, Esquire

Q: What do Clank and Bobble call Tinker Bell?

A: Miss Bell

Cody

First appearance:
The Rescuers Down Under (1990)

This brave little boy makes it his mission to save the wild animals in Australia from evil poachers. One day, he rescues the great golden eagle, Marahute, who is sought after by many a wicked hunter. But a poacher named Percival McLeach tricks Cody into leading him to Marahute's secret nest. Luckily, the Rescue Aid Society sends Bernard and Bianca to help Cody, and soon the little boy and Marahute are safe once and for all from McLeach.

Cool Quotes

"It's a trap! And poaching's against the law!"

"I'll never tell you where she is! Never! Never!"

Cody and Marahute

Colette

First appearance:
Disney • Pixar's Ratatouille (2007)

Colette is the only female chef at Gusteau's restaurant—and the toughest one, as well. Her skills with a knife are as fast and sharp as her tongue. At first, she's annoyed at being assigned to "babysit" Linguini when he starts working in the kitchen at Gusteau's. But before long, even Colette can't help enjoying her time coaching him.

Colette takes a listen to a fresh loaf.

Cool Quotes

"How do you tell great bread without tasting it? The sound!"

"Keep your station clear!"

"Let's cook!"

FUN FACT

Colette memorized every recipe created by her mentor, Chef Gusteau.

Copper

First appearance: The Fox and the Hound (1981)

When he was just a puppy, Copper the hound met a fox named Tod. The two became the best of friends. Later, Copper returns to his home and is trained to be a hunting dog. When he next meets Tod, the two are sworn enemies! Copper is confused and must decide how he will treat his old friend. Eventually, he realizes that a friendship like theirs is hard to find. He decides to let his pal go free . . . just as any good friend would do.

Tricky Trivia

Q: Who is Copper's owner?
A: Amos Slade

Tod and Copper love to play.

Cruella De Vil

First appearance:
101 Dalmatians *(1961)*

Cruella De Vil loves spots, spots, and more spots . . . and she'll do anything to get them. The "devil woman" goes as far as stealing Dalmatian puppies so that she can make a coat out of their spotted fur. Luckily, the clever little puppies have lots of dog friends and family members—as well as their own wits—to help them get out of Cruella's wicked grasp.

"Dognapping. Can you imagine?"

Did You Know ...?

Cruella doesn't steal all 101 Dalmatians. (She only steals 15 puppies. She buys the other 84 puppies. Pongo and Perdy make that a family of 101 when they rescue them all.)

Crush and Squirt

First appearance: Disney·Pixar's Finding Nemo (2003)

Thanks to this laid-back father-and-son pair and the rest of their sea turtle crew, Marlin and Dory make it to safety after their dangerous jellyfish encounter. Leading by example, Crush and Squirt also teach Marlin a little about parenting. When Squirt swims out into the mighty East Australian Current, Crush freely lets him go—something Marlin never would have thought to do with Nemo! Impressed, Marlin asks Crush how he knows when a child is ready to go out on their own, and the turtle coolly replies, "Well, you never really know. But when they know, you'll know. You know?"

Tricky Trivia

Q: How many years old is Crush?
A: 150

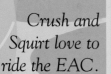

Crush and Squirt love to ride the EAC.

Cool Quotes

"No hurlin' on the shell, okay? Just waxed it." –Crush

"You rock, dude!" –Squirt

DAISY DUCK

First appearance: As "Donna Duck" in
Don Donald *(1937)*
As "Daisy Duck" in
Mr. Duck Steps Out *(1940)*

Daisy Duck is the sometimes patient, sometimes not-so-patient girlfriend of Donald Duck. Though she often puts up with Donald's antics and temper tantrums, she is also a strong character on her own. She loves flowers, shopping, and having fun with her best friend, Minnie Mouse. Donald is her one and only sweetheart, and always will be.

Daisy and Donald cut a rug!

FUN FACTS

LIKES
• Donald Duck
• The color pink
• Shopping

DISLIKES
• Donald's temper tantrums
• Having to wait

Dash and Violet Parr

First appearance:
Disney · Pixar's The Incredibles (2004)

Violet and Dash run for it.

Violet and Dash Parr may seem like typical siblings, but they each have unique Superpowers. Fourteen-year-old Violet can turn invisible and generate force fields, which not only helps her family triumph over the dastardly Syndrome, but also allows her to hide whenever she's feeling shy.

As for ten-year-old Dash, forget speeding bullets; he has the power to run faster than the speed of sound . . . and he's not afraid to use it! In fact, Dash doesn't understand why the Supers should have to hide their powers.

Tricky Trivia

Q: What is Dash's full name?

A: Dashiell Robert Parr

Q: What is Violet wearing at the end of *The Incredibles*?

A: A headband to keep her hair pushed back and out of her face.

Cool Quotes

"Normal? What does anyone in this family know about normal?!" –Violet

"I love our family!" –Dash

Django and Emile

First appearance:
Disney · Pixar's Ratatouille *(2007)*

Django and Emile love to eat junk food.

Remy's father and brother don't understand why Remy is so obsessed with gourmet food from the human world. Django wishes his son would follow in his paw-steps and one day become leader of their rat clan, and he just can't recognize what Remy sees in those untrustworthy humans. Emile would do anything for his brother, but he'll never quite get Remy's reluctance to eat perfectly good garbage. In the end, though, both rats stand by Remy and help him when he needs it the most.

Cool Quotes

"The key, my friend, is not to be picky."
–Emile

"It isn't stealing if no one wants it."
–Django

"We're not cooks, but we are family. You tell us what to do, and we'll get it done."
–Django

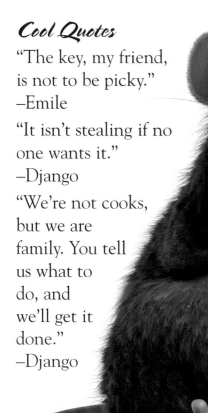

DONALD DUCK

First appearance:
The Wise Little Hen *(1934)*

Donald Duck is one hot-tempered fella. He always seems to be getting into some kind of trouble . . . and that's when his temper flares. And when Donald's angry, you can usually tell—he screams, *"Wak!"* and turns red in the face, and sometimes the feathers on his head stand straight up. So what are the causes of Donald's frustration? Sometimes it's his nephews playing tricks on him . . . or Goofy being clumsy . . . or some handsome rival flirting with his girlfriend, Daisy Duck. And other times, Donald just gets angry because of little things . . . like ants stealing his picnic lunch. Still, Donald has his happy moments. He's great pals with Mickey Mouse, and Daisy Duck will always be his sweetheart.

FUN FACT

As Walt Disney once said about Donald: "His towering rages, his impotence in the face of obstacles, his protests in the face of injustice, as he sees it—even though he brings disaster on himself—have kept him an audience favorite."

"Wak!"

COOL QUOTES

"Piece of cake!"

"Oh, boy! Oh, boy! Oh, boy!"

"Nothin' to it!"

Dory

First appearance:
Disney · Pixar's Finding Nemo *(2003)*

Throughout the vast ocean, you'll not find a fish friendlier, more hospitable, or more sociable than Dory. She'd love to chat with you all day and tell you her life story . . . though unfortunately, because she suffers from severe short-term memory loss, she can't. Still, she is the aquatic do-gooder who offers to help a clownfish named Marlin on his journey to find his son, Nemo, and her enduring optimism plays no small part in his success.

"Just keep swimming!"

Tricky Trivia

Q: What kind of fish is Dory?

A: A regal blue tang

Cool Quote

"I forget things almost instantly. It runs in my family. . . . Well, I mean, at least I think it does. Umm . . . hmm . . . where are they? . . . Can I help you?"

FUN FACTS

- Dory can read Human and speak Whale.
- Comedian Ellen DeGeneres provided the voice for Dory.

Dot

First appearance:
Disney•Pixar's A Bug's Life (1998)

Spunky and tomboyish, the adorable Princess Dot is full of mischief, and often is frustrated at playing second fiddle to her older sister, the soon-to-be-queen, Atta. However, Dot's energy seems to find an outlet in Flik, the bumbling and brilliant inventor ant, who also happens to have a huge crush on Atta. When Flik is down and out, it is Princess Dot who believes in him and inspires him to achieve greatness.

Flik and Dot

Cool Quote

When Flik tells Dot to imagine that the rock he is holding is really a seed, Dot replies, "But it's a rock."

Duchess

(and Berlioz, Toulouse & Marie)

First appearance: The Aristocats (1970)

Duchess and her three little kittens belong to Madame Bonfamille, who spoils her felines and makes sure that Duchess encourages the little ones' talents. Marie, the only girl, is white and likes to wear pink bows. Toulouse is orange with a blue bow tie, and often ready for mischief. Berlioz is dark gray and is always picking fights with his siblings. Madame Bonfamille plans on leaving her entire (large) fortune to her cats. This, of course, makes her butler, Edgar, very jealous, and that's where the adventure begins!

An evening outing

DUG AND KEVIN

First appearance:
Disney·Pixar's Up (2009)

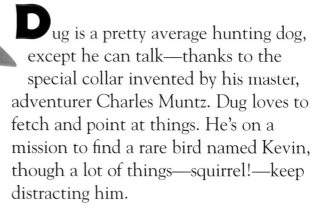

Dug is a pretty average hunting dog, except he can talk—thanks to the special collar invented by his master, adventurer Charles Muntz. Dug loves to fetch and point at things. He's on a mission to find a rare bird named Kevin, though a lot of things—squirrel!—keep distracting him.

Kevin is a twelve-foot-tall jungle bird. She can't say a word, but she is the object of Charles Muntz's obsession. According to Muntz, her species used to roam all over the Earth and is the missing link between dinosaurs and birds. Now, however, Kevin hides out in her rocky labyrinth, caring for her babies and emerging only to look for food.

TRICKY TRIVIA

Q: How does Charles Muntz punish Dug for losing track of Kevin?

A: He makes Dug wear the Cone of Shame.

Q: What is Kevin's favorite food?

A: Chocolate

DUMBO

First appearance: Dumbo (1941)

When Dumbo is first delivered via stork to Mrs. Jumbo, the baby elephant seems perfect in every way . . . until he sneezes and reveals his giant ears. Luckily, Dumbo's mother loves her son just the way he is. Then one terrible day, a mean boy mocks Dumbo. When Mrs. Jumbo defends her son, she ends up in jail and is labeled a mad and dangerous elephant. Dumbo is heartbroken and misses his mother terribly. But soon he is befriended by the kindhearted and circus-savvy Timothy Mouse, who helps Dumbo gain confidence in himself. In the end, Dumbo's ears prove to be truly extraordinary— they help him to fly! This brings little Dumbo fame and fortune, and allows him to be reunited with his beloved mother.

FUN FACTS

- When Dumbo is first delivered, his mother, Mrs. Jumbo, names him Jumbo Jr.
- Dumbo never speaks.

"You're standing on the threshold of success!"

E (aka Edna Mode)
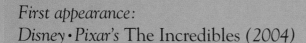

First appearance:
Disney·Pixar's The Incredibles *(2004)*

Brilliant and successful, E (aka Edna Mode) got her start in the fashion industry as the world's leading costume designer for the Supers. Of course, once the Supers had to go into hiding, she took her talents to the world of high-end fashion and soon became the top name in design. E's passion, however, will always be in combining the latest in textile technology with her impeccable sense of style to create the world's most incredible—and wearable—Super suits.

A new Super suit is in order.

Cool Quotes

"Words are useless. Gobble, gobble, gobble. There is too much of it, dahling. That is why I show you my work."

"I never look back, dahling. It distracts from the now."

"No capes. Now go on. Your next suit will be finished before your next assignment."

Eeyore

First appearance: Winnie the Pooh and the Honey Tree (1966)

Eeyore and friends

"Looks like rain." Or at least that's what Eeyore would say (even on a sunny day). Eeyore is so gloomy, he speaks in a deep monotone and hardly has the energy to form complete sentences. Still, Eeyore is a good friend, and will do practically anything to help out his pals in the Hundred-Acre Wood.

Some gloomier aspects of Eeyore's life

- His house is a stick tepee that lets in wind, rain, and snow.
- His favorite snack is prickly thistles.

Some happier aspects of Eeyore's life

- He is loved by all his friends. In fact, Christopher Robin once gave a hero party in his honor (or at least that's what Eeyore thought).
- He some-times has a positive attitude: "Coulda been worse."

Elastigirl
(aka Helen Parr)

First appearance:
Disney·Pixar's The Incredibles (2004)

Elastigirl sure can stretch!

Adjusting to "normal" life was no problem for Elastigirl (aka Helen Parr) when the government forced the Supers to go into hiding. After all, raising three kids and running a household can keep a person pretty busy. Plus, she could still use her amazing ability to stretch her body to meet the daily challenges of modern motherhood—as long as it was in secret. But when her family's safety was threatened, Elastigirl jumped at the chance to get back into full Super mode and come to the rescue!

Cool Quotes

"Leave the saving of the world to the men? I don't think so!"

"We are not going to die! Now both of you will get a grip, or so help me I'll ground you for a month!"
–Helen, talking to her children, Dash and Violet

Esmeralda

First appearance:
The Hunchback of Notre Dame (1996)

Esmeralda is one of the first and only people to show kindness to the Hunchback of Notre Dame, Quasimodo, who falls in love with the beautiful gypsy. Even though Esmeralda doesn't love Quasimodo in return (she is truly in love with the soldier Phoebus), she does help him gain the confidence he needs in order to get out from under the grasp of his evil master, Frollo.

Tricky Trivia

Q: What's the name of Esmeralda's pet goat?

A: Djali (pronounced "jolly")

Q: What is on the pendant that Esmeralda gives to Quasimodo?

A: A map to the secret place where the gypsies live, so he can find her if he needs her.

Esmeralda, Quasimodo, and Phoebus enjoy the view.

EVE

First appearance:
Disney • Pixar's WALL•E *(2008)*

Pure white, egg-shaped, graceful—and fully armed!—EVE is by far the most beautiful thing WALL•E has ever seen when she lands on his trash-filled planet. WALL•E wants nothing more than to hold her "hand," but EVE is on a mission to scout out living plant life on Earth in order to determine whether it is capable of supporting human life. When she finds a plant (thanks to WALL•E), nothing stops her from accomplishing her directive. She soon discovers, though, how valuable friendship can be.

Tricky Trivia

Q: What does "EVE" stand for?

A: Extraterrestrial Vegetation Evaluator

Q: What is the name of the massive spaceship EVE is sent from?

A: The Axiom

EVE wants WALL•E to go back to Earth.

60

The Fairy Godmother

First appearance: Cinderella (1950)

Where would Cinderella be without her Fairy Godmother? This loving, (though absentminded) magical Fairy Godmother appears in Cinderella's life just when the girl has given up all hope for happiness. The Fairy Godmother waves her magic wand, says the magic words, and Cinderella's special night comes alive. She is the one character (aside from Cinderella's animal friends) who is kind to Cinderella in her time of need.

The Fairy Godmother works her magic!

FUN FACT

The Fairy Godmother almost sends Cinderella to the ball with a coach, four horses, a coachman, a footman . . . and no gown!

Fawn, Iridessa, Rosetta, Silvermist, and Vidia

First appearance: Tinker Bell (2008)

Vidia blames Tink for her sticky situation.

These fairies are not only Tinker Bell's friends, but they are among the most gifted of their various talent groups.

- Quite the adventurer, animal fairy Fawn can communicate with any living creature.
- Light fairy Iridessa has a sparkling personality and can shape, bend, and create light.

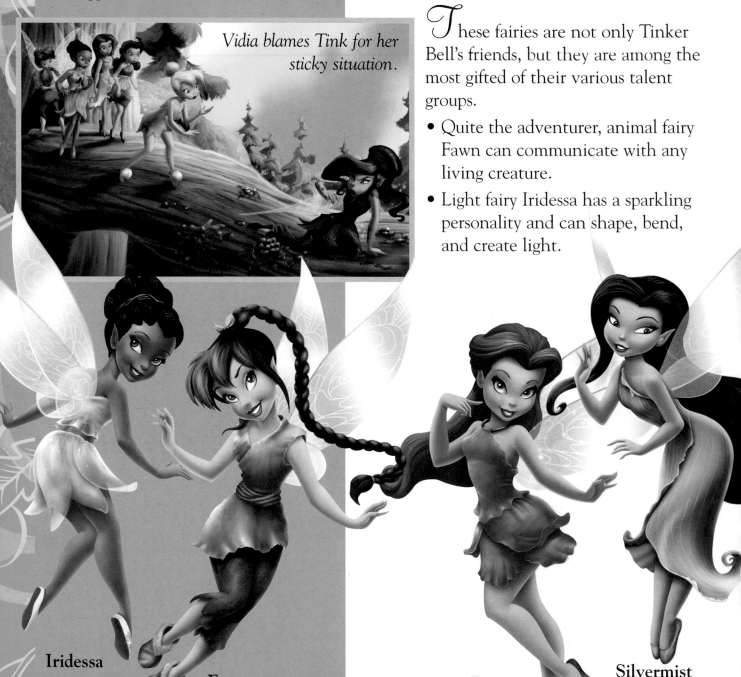

Iridessa

Fawn

Rosetta

Silvermist

Tink can fix anything!

- Garden fairy Rosetta nurtures the flowers in Pixie Hollow and approaches everyone with her sweet charm.

- As a water fairy, Silvermist can control and manipulate water as if it were something solid. She is also often the first in line to lend a hand.

- Vidia, the fastest of all the fast-flying fairies, is selfish and impatient with her fellow fairies, but she has been known to come through for them in the end.

Cool Quotes

"It's all right. Fawn's got 'ya."
–Fawn, calming Cheese the mouse

"It might be the sparkliest thing I've ever seen. And I've seen a lot of sparkly things!"
–Iridessa

"Oh, sweet pea, I think this is your talent." –Rosetta, talking to Tink

"If at first you don't succeed, fly, fly again!" –Silvermist

"Fairies of every talent depend on me." –Vidia

Vidia

Queen Clarion scolds Vidia.

Did You Know ...?

The fairies live in Pixie Hollow. Fawn lives in a pine tree, Iridessa lives in a sunflower, Rosetta lives in a house made of buttercups, Silvermist lives by a waterfall, and Vidia lives by herself in a sour-plum tree.

Figaro and Cleo

First appearance: Pinocchio (1940)

Figaro the cat and Cleo the goldfish are Geppetto's only friends before Pinocchio enters his life. The cute little black-and-white kitten, Figaro, has a feisty side. When Geppetto finishes making Pinocchio and begins to play with the marionette, Figaro becomes downright jealous. When the puppet "touches" him, the cat even fights back by batting at him, claws and all. Cleo, on the other hand, is clearly a pampered little beauty of a goldfish. Every night, she rolls over in her bowl to allow Geppetto to gently tickle her belly. Both she and Figaro adore Geppetto and are incredibly loyal to him. They even go with him on his search for the lost Pinocchio, all the way into Monstro the Whale's belly and back home again, where Pinocchio at last becomes a real boy.

Pinocchio comes to life!

Flik

*First appearance: Disney•Pixar's
A Bug's Life (1998)*

This goofy and brilliant worker ant seems to be able to do nothing but get his colony into deeper and deeper trouble. When he invents a machine to help the ants harvest grain faster, it only ends up knocking their entire collection of grain into the riverbed. This puts the ant colony in a terrible position when the bullying grasshoppers come to collect the grain. In order to make up for his mistake, Flik sets out to find some warrior bugs to help defend the ant colony against the mean grasshoppers. He unknowingly brings home a bunch of circus bugs instead. In the end, the circus bugs actually turn into heroes—as does Flik himself!

Tricky Trivia

Q: Who is the one ant who believes in Flik at the beginning of the movie?

A: Dot

Q: How does Flik manage to fly away from Ant Island?

A: On a dandelion seed

Flik is ready for adventure!

Flora, Fauna, & Merryweather

First appearance: Sleeping Beauty (1959)

These three good fairies first come into Princess Aurora's life when she is born, and they raise her in a cottage in the forest as Briar Rose until her sixteenth birthday. Their mission is to care for the growing child and protect her from the evil fairy, Maleficent, and her wicked curse. They accomplish both goals almost completely—their only mistake is that on the very last day that Maleficent's curse might hold any power, they use their magic.

Unfortunately, this releases magical sparkles up the cottage's chimney, thus revealing their hiding place to Maleficent. The evil fairy then tricks the young princess into pricking her finger on a spinning wheel, activating the terrible curse Maleficent had placed on her at birth. The good fairies race to the rescue, putting everyone to sleep and helping Prince Phillip battle Maleficent by giving him the Shield of Virtue and the Sword of Truth. When Phillip triumphs over the evil fairy, the good fairies lift the sleeping spell and allow the brave prince to kiss the Sleeping Beauty, awakening her from her cursed sleep.

Merryweather (blue),
Fauna (green),
and Flora (red)

Tricky Trivia

Q: Do you remember which gift each fairy bestows upon the infant Princess Aurora?

A: Flora gives her beauty, Fauna gives her the gift of song, and Merryweather gives her the chance to have Maleficent's curse undone by the kiss of true love.

Flora, Fauna, and Merryweather can perform magic like the best of fairies, but when it comes to baking a cake and sewing a dress for Briar Rose's sixteenth birthday, they are completely incompetent!

The fairies give Prince Phillip the Sword of Truth.

Q: When the fairies use their magic to create a dress for Briar Rose's sixteenth birthday, what difference of opinion causes an argument between Merryweather and Flora?

A: Merryweather wants the dress to be blue; Flora wants it to be pink.

Flounder

First appearance:
The Little Mermaid (1989)

Though he's sometimes reluctant to follow his more adventurous friend Ariel, Flounder always seems to be at the Little Mermaid's side, through thick and thin. He goes with her when she explores sunken ships (against her father's will)—even when there are sharks lurking nearby. Later, when Ariel is human and cannot swim, it is Flounder who helps her get out to Prince Eric's ship in order to save the prince and the entire undersea kingdom.

Cool Quotes from Flounder

"Do you really think there might be sharks around here?"

"This is great. I mean, I really, uh, love this excitement . . . adventure . . . danger lurking. . . ."

Cool Quote about Flounder

"Flounder, you really are a guppy!"
(Ariel teasing Flounder for being scared)

Sebastian is not amused!

Flower

First appearance: Bambi (1942)

Flower the skunk is one of the first friends Bambi meets in the forest. When Flower hibernates for the winter, Bambi cannot understand why his little pal is too sleepy to go out to play.

Flower gets his name when young Bambi is learning his first words. He learns the word *flower.* Then, when the little skunk pops his head out from among the flowers Bambi is exploring, the fawn calls him "Flower," too. The name sticks.

Bambi meets Flower for the first time.

69

Gaston

First appearance:
Beauty and the Beast (1991)

The arrogant bachelor Gaston wants nothing more than to marry Belle, but the bookish beauty has no interest in him . . . at all. This, of course, astounds Gaston. How could any eligible young woman not want to marry a handsome, athletic hunter such as himself?

Still, though Gaston seems like nothing but a self-absorbed nuisance at first, his jealousy and rage take a dangerous turn, and he ends up leading an angry crowd of villagers to kill the Beast. (Luckily, the Beast battles back and, with some help from Belle, manages to defeat the villain.)

Arrogant Quotes

"It's about time you got your head out of those books and paid attention to important things—like me."

"I'll have Belle for my wife. Make no mistake about it."

"I'd like to thank you all for coming to my wedding. First, I better go in there and propose to the girl!"

Gaston and his men storm the castle.

Genie

First appearance: Aladdin (1992)

He's big. He's blue. And he's constantly changing. In fact, you never know quite what you're going to get with Aladdin's Genie. He changes voices, characters, and even body shapes. But usually you can tell who he is: he's the most outrageous personality in the room.

Cool Quotes

"It never fails— get in the bath, there's a rub at the lamp."

"Ten thousand years will give you *such* a crick in the neck!"

"I'm getting kind of fond of you, kid. Not that I wanna pick out curtains or anything."

"Hello, Aladdin. Nice to have you on the show. Can we call you 'Al'? Or maybe just 'Din'? Or how about 'Laddie'?"

To the Magic Carpet: "Rugman! Haven't seen you in a fewmillennia. Give me some tassel!"

He's the genie of 1,000 faces!

FUN FACT

Comedian Robin Williams provided the voice of Genie.

Georgette

First appearance:
Oliver & Company (1988)

Georgette is a pampered poodle who lives a life of ease with her owner, Jenny. However, when Oliver comes to live in the house, Georgette becomes so jealous that she wants to get rid of the little kitten. Luckily, though, Jenny loves Oliver and will do anything to keep him, even if it means battling vicious kidnappers to rescue him. In the end, Georgette learns to put up with Oliver . . . although she probably will never be his biggest fan.

Did You Know . . . ?

Pongo makes a cameo appearance in *Oliver & Company*. (He appears in a busy street scene, walking on the sidewalk.)

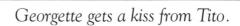

Georgette gets a kiss from Tito.

Geppetto

First appearance: Pinocchio (1940)

Geppetto the wood-carver lives a fairly ordinary life with his pet goldfish, Cleo, and his cat, Figaro. But when he makes a little wooden puppet and then wishes that the puppet would be brought to life, Geppetto's life changes dramatically. The little wooden boy, of course, does come to life . . . and ends up causing poor Geppetto a lot of heartache before becoming a real boy at last.

Geppetto puts the finishing touches on Pinocchio.

Geppetto's Wish:

"Star light, star bright,
First star I see tonight.
I wish I may, I wish I might . . .
Have the wish I make tonight."

"Figaro, you know what I wished? I wished that my little Pinocchio might be a real boy!"

FUN FACT

When Geppetto is swallowed by Monstro the Whale, he gets his food by fishing inside the whale's belly!

Gideon and J. Worthington Foulfellow

First appearance: Pinocchio (1940)

Pinocchio walks right into a trap!

Gideon is the silly sidekick cat to the nasty fox, J. Worthington Foulfellow—usually known as Honest John. The two trick Pinocchio into skipping school in order to join a traveling theater group. Later, they fool the little puppet into going off to Pleasure Island, where he barely escapes being transformed into a donkey and sold into a life of labor.

Not-So-Cool Quote

When Honest John tries to lure Pinocchio into a life of acting, the fox says, "Why, I can see your name in lights. Lights six feet high! Uh, what's your name?"

Giselle

First appearance: Enchanted (2007)

Giselle is the ideal fairy-tale heroine—lovely, kind, and forever optimistic. She dreams of nothing more than meeting a handsome prince and living happily ever after. Unfortunately, her handsome prince has a wicked stepmother, Queen Narissa, who's willing to do anything to keep her stepson from marrying and taking over the royal throne. Narissa goes so far as to disguise herself as an old hag and push Giselle down a wishing well and into the real world of New York City. Once there, Giselle fears that her happy dreams are over . . . but she soon finds out that waking up to real life can be even more magical and fun.

Tricky Trivia

Q: What is the name of the fairy-tale kingdom that Giselle comes from?

A: Andalasia

Giselle falls through a magic portal.

GOOFY

First appearance:
Mickey's Revue (1932)

Beloved by mostof his friends (except Donald Duck, who finds Goofy's antics to be highly irritating), Goofy is fun-loving and . . . yes, goofy. He is constantly doing something clumsy that causes him to be stuck in some sort of awkward situation. But never fear—Goofy may be a klutz, but he'll easily bounce back from almost any predicament without a scratch.

GOOFY-ISMS

"Gawrsh!"
"A-hyuck!"
"Whoopsy. Sorry."
"Whoa!"

Under the deep blue sea

FUN FACTS

- When Goofy's son Max goes to college (in *An Extremely Goofy Movie*), Goofy decides to go, too!
- The character we know as Goofy was originally called "Dippy Dawg."

Hades

First appearance: Hercules (1997)

He's mean. He's angry. And he's plenty jealous of Zeus. The evil Hades, lord of the Underworld, is in a funk over a spat he had with Zeus—a spat that led Zeus to kick the evil god off Mount Olympus and down into the Underworld, where he serves as lord of the dead. Now Hades is out to get Zeus's son, Hercules. Luckily, good always triumphs over evil!

Tricky Trivia

Q: When Hades is battling Zeus and the other gods and goddesses, what superpowers does he call upon to help him?

A: The Titans, who were long ago imprisoned by Zeus for their evil deeds

Q: What are the names of Hades' sidekicks who kidnap Hercules from his home on Olympus?

A: Pain and Panic

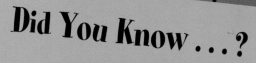

Did You Know . . . ?

In ancient Greece, citizens worshipped a group of gods and goddesses ruled by Zeus.

"And here's a sucker for the little sucker."

Hercules

First appearance: Hercules (1997)

As the son of Zeus (the ruler of all the Greek gods), Hercules becomes a hero on earth. Raised by adoptive human parents, Hercules grows up an awkward and gawky boy. When he discovers that he is part god and part mortal, he goes into hero training where he learns to channel his energy. But his greatest test comes when the evil Hades drains Hercules of his godlike strength. Then Hercules must use true heroics to overcome the odds. He even saves all of the gods and goddesses as he defeats the wicked Hades. In the end, though, Hercules decides he would rather not become a god (though he has finally earned the right to join them). He would prefer to stay on earth with his one true (human) love, Meg.

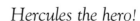

Hercules the hero!

FUN FACTS

Likes
- Meg
- Working out
- Fighting for good

Dislikes
- Hades
- Evil

HUEY, DEWEY, AND LOUIE

First appearance:
Donald's Nephews *(1938)*

Huey, Dewey, and Louie are Donald Duck's mischievous nephews. These three little guys are always getting into trouble because of their sense of adventure and good fun—and Donald constantly gets into fixes due to their antics. Luckily for Huey, Dewey, and Louie, they also can turn on the charm and be absolutely adorable. So, even after they've tangled Uncle Donald up in his hammock or played some practical joke on him, they usually end up in Donald's good graces.

Did You Know . . . ?

Here's how you can tell which nephew is which:

- Huey wears red. (Just remember that red is the brightest *hue*.)
- Dewey wears blue. (Think of *dew*, which is water, which sometimes looks blue.)
- Louie wears green. (*Louie* begins with the letter *L*, just like *leaves*, which are green!)

Jasmine

First appearance: Aladdin (1992)

Born into royalty (she's the daughter of the Sultan), Jasmine is tough, smart . . . and a little bit lonely. Her biggest problem is that she is required to marry before her next birthday, but she doesn't want to marry a royal snob. She wants to find a husband she can love. Jasmine also feels trapped in the palace and wants to be free to make her own choices. After sneaking out one day, she runs into some trouble in the marketplace. A street rat named Aladdin saves her from the royal guards and takes her to his hideout in the rooftops. Jasmine likes him right away, but Aladdin feels that he'll never impress her in his rags.

When Aladdin comes to the palace as Prince Ali Ababwa, Jasmine is not amused. She thinks that Prince Ali is just like all the other stuck-up suitors who

Jasmine speaks her mind.

have tried to win her hand. But then Prince Ali takes Jasmine on a magic carpet ride, and she begins to see that there's a kind and loving heart beneath his phony robes. After Jafar steals the magic lamp and reveals that Ali is really Aladdin, Jasmine feels betrayed. But Aladdin proves his courage by saving Jasmine and defeating the evil vizier. Her love for Aladdin is so strong, that it convinces her father to change the law that requires her to marry a prince.

Tricky Trivia

Q: Who is Jasmine's best friend before she meets Aladdin?

A: Her pet tiger, Rajah

Q: How does Jasmine distract Jafar when he takes the magic lamp?

A: She kisses him!

Cool Quotes

"I am not a prize to be won."
"I choose you, Aladdin."

Jasmine longs to be independent.

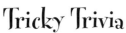

FUN FACT Jasmine's singing voice was provided by Lea Salonga, the award-winning actress who played the lead in "Miss Saigon" on Broadway. But Jasmine isn't the only Disney heroine who sings with Lea's beautiful voice—Mulan's songs were performed by Lea, too!

Jasmine has eyes only for Aladdin.

JESSIE

First appearance:
Disney • Pixar's Toy Story 2 (1999)

When Woody is toynapped by the toy collector Al McWhiggin, he soon realizes that he was once the star of his own TV show, *Woody's Roundup*. One of his costars on the show was Jessie, the yodeling cowgirl. Woody meets Jessie in Al's apartment, and the two begin a wonderful friendship. Jessie tells Woody that he should live the life of a collectible toy because kids like Andy grow up—the way her owner did, eventually leaving Jessie behind. Luckily, Woody decides to stay with Andy anyway, and he even brings Jessie home with him where she learns to love and be loved once again by a real, live kid.

COOL QUOTES

"It's you! It's you! It's you, it's you, it's you!"

"Sweet mother of Abraham Lincoln!"

"Oh, Bullseye, we're part of a family again!"

Jessie and Bullseye are one half of the Roundup gang.

Jim Hawkins

First appearance: Treasure Planet (2002)

Jim Hawkins is a talented fifteen-year-old boy who lives on the planet Montressor. He loves solar-surfing, and often spends his time helping his mother run the Benbow Inn. When he receives a stern warning from local law enforcement after solar-surfing in a restricted area, it looks as if Jim may be headed for bigger trouble. However, his life is about to change. A grizzled alien named Billy Bones crash-lands his ship near the Benbow Inn and, with his dying gasp, hands Jim a mysterious sphere. Jim soon realizes he has been given the map to the long-lost Treasure Planet—the one and only place where the notorious pirate Captain Nathaniel Flint hid his famous "loot of a thousand worlds." Jim soon embarks on the adventure of a lifetime, and along the way, learns about friendship, loss, and the sweet victory of finding true treasure: belief in oneself.

Tricky Trivia

Q: Why is Jim crucial to the pirates when they are trying to find Flint's treasure?

A: Jim has the treasure map, and he's the only one who knows how to use it.

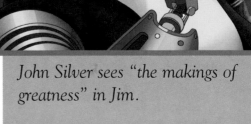

John Silver sees "the makings of greatness" in Jim.

Jiminy Cricket

First appearance: Pinocchio (1940)

Little did Jiminy Cricket know what he was in for when he first entered Geppetto's workshop for a warm night's sleep. Soon after the cricket arrived, Geppetto finished carving a little wooden puppet named Pinocchio. That night, Pinocchio was brought to life by the Blue Fairy, who immediately assigned Jiminy the job of being Pinocchio's conscience.

Cool Quote

"Temptations. They're the wrong things that seem right at the time. But, uh, even though right things may seem wrong sometimes, eh, sometimes the wrong things (ha!) may be right at the wrong time. Or, eh, vice versa. Ha-ha! Understand?"

Jiminy looks like one cranky cricket!

FUN FACT

As Pinocchio's conscience, Jiminy's official job title is "Lord High Keeper of the Knowledge of Right and Wrong, Counselor in Moments of Temptation, and Guide along the Straight and Narrow Path."

John Smith

First appearance: Pocahontas (1995)

John Smith is an adventurer at heart. He's the first to jump ashore when his ship arrives at the New World, and he is the first to explore the woods alone. When he meets Pocahontas, he grows to love her . . . and to understand her culture despite their different backgrounds. Together, John Smith and Pocahontas work to bring peace between their people as a war begins to break out around them. Risking their lives, they accomplish this goal, and peace returns to Pocahontas's native land.

Pocahontas teaches John Smith to respect nature.

Cool Quote

"I'd rather die tomorrow than live a hundred years without knowing you." (John Smith to Pocahontas)

JUMBA & PLEAKLEY

First appearance: Lilo & Stitch (2002)

Not your typical tourists!

Okay—for starters, Jumba Jukiba is the scientist who created Stitch (calling him "Experiment 626"). And Pleakley thinks he's an expert on the planet Earth, based on the knowledge he's gained from looking at pictures from an old View-Master. For some reason, the Grand Councilwoman assigns these two to go to Earth to retrieve the escaped convict, Experiment 626. The two not-so-cleverly disguise themselves as tourists and set out to capture Stitch. The only problem is that Jumba is out for revenge, and Pleakley is just following orders.

COOL QUOTES

"Earth is a protected wildlife preserve. Yeah. We've been using it to rebuild the mosquito population, which—need I remind you?—is an endangered species!" (Pleakley to the Grand Councilwoman)

"Don't run! Don't make me shoot you! You were expensive." (Jumba to Stitch)

Kaa

First appearance: The Jungle Book (1967)

This pesky python has a very bad lisp, which often makes his speech sound like hissing—especially because he tends to use lots of words that begin with the letter *s*! He would like nothing better than to make a meal of Mowgli, and he tries his utmost to wrap his coils around the Man-cub. Kaa also has the ability to hypnotize his victims using his spellbinding stare. Like most slithering serpents, he is very sly, but he is also terrified of the jungle's biggest villain: Shere Khan.

Did You Know . . . ?

The actor who provided the voice of Kaa, Sterling Holloway, lent his vocal talents to many Disney films. He voiced the character of Pooh in *Winnie the Pooh and the Blustery Day* (1968), *Winnie the Pooh and Tigger Too* (1974), and *The Many Adventures of Winnie the Pooh* (1977). He also supplied the voice of Roquefort in *The Aristocats*!

Kaa tries to trap Mowgli in his coils.

Kanga and Roo

First appearance: Winnie the Pooh and the Honey Tree *(1966)*

FUN FACTS

- Kanga is the only one in the Hundred-Acre Wood who can make Tigger feel shy (when she calls him "dear").
- Kanga is the only female among the main inhabitants of the Hundred-Acre Wood.

Kanga is little Roo's mother. (Together, their names spell, appropriately, *kangaroo*.) Warm and caring, she always makes sure that Roo is bathed, fed, and kept out of danger. Roo loves his mama, but he also loves bouncing and spending time with Tigger, too.

tricky trivia

Q: Where does Roo sleep?
A: In his bed! (No, he doesn't sleep in Kanga's pouch!)
Q: When Kanga first moved to the Hundred-Acre Wood, why were Rabbit and the others afraid of her?
A: They saw Roo jump into her pouch, and they thought she had eaten him!

Flowers for mama

Kenai and Koda

First appearance: Brother Bear (2003)

The bears at the salmon run

Headstrong teenager Kenai was upset with the Great Spirits—after all, they had allowed a bear to kill his brother. But he got really angry when they turned him into a bear!

When Kenai met a little cub named Koda, he wanted nothing to do with him. With time, though, Kenai realized how much they had in common, and the two bears became as close as real brothers. In fact, when Kenai finally had the chance to become human again, he chose to remain a bear and look after his orphaned cub friend.

Tricky Trivia

Q: What does Kenai's bear totem symbolize?

A: Love

Cool Quotes

"He does a lotta weird stuff! Like the way he drinks water from a leaf . . . He's never even sharpened his claws on a tree . . . He's never hibernated before . . . He doesn't know how to lick himself clean . . ."–Koda, talking about Kenai

Kida

First appearance:
Atlantis: The Lost Empire *(2001)*

Kida lends Milo a helping hand.

Princess Kida lost her mother to the mysterious Atlantean Crystal when she was just a little girl. It turns out the powerful Crystal needed to take someone of royal birth in order to save Atlantis from destruction. Later, when Milo and his fellow explorers rediscover Atlantis, Princess Kida is as curious to learn from Milo as he is to learn from her. Together, they grow to understand their different worlds—and save Atlantis from another threat of destruction. This time it is Kida who joins with the mysterious Crystal to save her city and her people. Luckily, unlike her mother before her, Kida is returned to Atlantis—and Milo— by the Crystal.

Tricky Trivia

Q: What is Kida's full name?

A: Princess Kidagakash

Q: How old is Kida?

A: About 8,400 years old, which is only about 28 human years (Atlanteans live 300 years for every one year of human life.)

KRONK

First appearance:
The Emperor's New Groove (2000)

Kronk is Yzma's right-hand guy. He may not be very bright, but he's a really good cook. Unfortunately for Yzma, this combination gets her into a lot

Kronk listens to his conscience(s).

of trouble. When Yzma tries to get rid of the emperor, she invites him to dinner—and leaves it up to Kronk to prepare the meal and put a potion in Kuzco's drink. But Kronk gets confused, and Kuzco is accidentally turned into a llama. Still, Kronk proves to be rather useful—carrying Yzma through the jungle in a litter, helping her track down Kuzco by speaking Squirrel (to a squirrel), and even cooking for her. What else could a royal pain like Yzma ask for?

Tricky Trivia

Q: When did Kronk learn to speak Squirrel?

A: When he was a Junior Chipmunk

KUZCO

First appearance:
The Emperor's New Groove (2000)

This emperor with an attitude learns a lot about life when he gets turned into a llama. He loses his job, his identity, and his supersnobby attitude . . . which actually works out for the best for everybody. He learns the most, though, from a simple peasant named Pacha, whose biggest goal in life is to keep his family happy and healthy. When Kuzco finally becomes emperor again—with Pacha's help—he rules with a much kinder, humbler hand.

Cool Quotes

"Boo-yah!"
"No touchy!"
"Cha!"
"Ba-boom, baby!"

FUN FACT

Kuzco also turns into a turtle, a bird, and a whale.

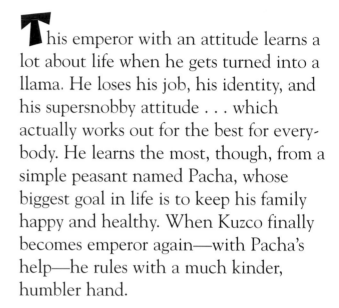

"Oh, yeah."

Lady and Tramp

First appearance: Lady and the Tramp (1955)

Lady isn't sure what to make of Tramp when he first comes into her well-groomed yard. Tramp is a mutt from the other side of town. He has no home and no family, unlike Lady, who lives with Jim Dear and Darling. However, after Tramp rescues Lady from the mean Aunt Sarah and then takes her to a romantic dinner at Tony's Restaurant, Lady finds herself falling in love. The two are a perfect match, and soon enough, Tramp comes to live in Lady's home for the rest of their happy lives together.

Tramp's Trivia

Q: What does Tramp call Lady?

A: Pidge

Q: How does Tramp manage to get rid of Lady's muzzle?

A: He tricks a beaver into thinking the muzzle is a log carrier. Then the beaver gets the muzzle off Lady.

An unlikely pair

Lady Tremaine

First appearance: Cinderella (1950)

It is Cinderella's unfortunate fate that her father takes the cruel and wicked Lady Tremaine as his second wife. Along with her nasty daughters, Anastasia and Drizella, Lady Tremaine makes Cinderella a prisoner in her own home after her father's death. Condescending and rude, Lady Tremaine forces Cinderella to cook, clean the stately château where they live, and wait on her and her daughters hand and foot.

Mirror, mirror on the wall, who's the meanest stepmother of all?

FUN FACT

Lady Tremaine doesn't realize that Cinderella was at the ball until she overhears Cinderella humming the tune she danced to the night before. Lady Tremaine puts two and two together, and figures out that Cinderella is the girl for whom the Prince is searching.

94

Lewis

First appearance: Meet the Robinsons (2007)

Twelve-year-old Lewis, it seems, can invent just about anything, but he can't seem to find a family to adopt him. So he decides to build a Memory Scanner, which can at least help him remember the mother that left him at the orphanage door so many years ago. But before Lewis can make the thing work, the villainous Bowler Hat Guy sabotages it. Then a boy named Wilbur (who says he's a time cop) transports Lewis to the future. There, Lewis ends up meeting the family of his dreams who, as it turns out, will be his own family one day!

FUN FACT

Lewis's motto when he grows up, "Keep moving forward," comes from a quotation from Walt Disney himself: "Around here, we don't look backwards for very long. We keep moving forward, opening up new doors, and doing new things, because we're curious . . . and curiosity keeps leading us down new paths."

Tricky Trivia

Q: What year in the future does Lewis travel to?

A: 2037

Q: What does Lewis change his name to when he grows up?

A: Cornelius Robinson

Lewis, the inventor

Lightning McQueen

First appearance:
Disney · Pixar's Cars (2006)

Poised to win the Piston Cup championship, Lightning McQueen has just two things on his mind: winning and the perks that come with it. But when he gets lost in the forgotten town of Radiator Springs and has to re-pave the main street (which he accidentally ruined), he's suddenly forced to rethink everything. Thanks to the cars that Lightning meets there, he soon discovers that friendship and teamwork are more important than winning and fame. (Though he still likes to win, of course!)

Cool Quotes

"Ka-chow!"

"I am speed."

Tricky Trivia

Q: What is the name of the championship race for the Piston Cup?

A: Dinoco 400

Q: Who is Lightning's major sponsor?

A: Rust-eze Medicated Bumper Ointment

FUN FACT

Lightning McQueen's number, 95, is the same year (1995) that the movie *Toy Story*, Pixar's first feature film, was released.

Lightning hits the road.

LILO

First appearance: Lilo & Stitch (2002)

Stitch's badness level is unusually high.

When Lilo wishes on a falling star and asks for a friend, the little Hawaiian girl does not realize that the "falling star" is really a spaceship from outer space . . . and that it contains a genetic experiment gone wrong. Uh-oh. Soon Lilo adopts "Experiment 626," thinking the creature is a dog, and she names him Stitch. Over time, she teaches Stitch all about 'ohana, and the little guy actually tosses aside his wild ways in order to become a part of Lilo's family.

LILO'S RITUALS

Lilo feeds Pudge the fish a peanut butter sandwich every Thursday (because, she says, he controls the weather).

COOL QUOTES

"Dad said 'ohana means family. Family means nobody gets left behind—or forgotten."

"I'm sorry I bit you. And pulled your hair. And punched you in the face."

"Stitch is troubled. He needs desserts."

"He used to be a collie before he got run over."

Linguini

First appearance:
Disney·Pixar's Ratatouille (2007)

When Linguini first arrives at Gusteau's restaurant with a letter of reference from his late mother, he has no idea that he's really the long-lost son of the world-famous chef. All he wants is a simple job, but a chance encounter with a rat named Remy thrusts him into the gourmet spotlight. Linguini soon finds himself the leader of the kitchen (with Remy secretly directing his cooking from under his chef's toque).

Cool Quotes

"We can be the greatest restaurant in Paris, and this rat can lead us there!"

"So let's do this thing!"

Tricky Trivia

Q: How does Remy control Linguini's actions in the kitchen?

A: By pulling his hair

Q: What is the first recipe of Gusteau's that Linguini is asked to make?

A: Sweetbreads á la Gusteau

Linguini takes notes in the kitchen.

Little John

First appearance: Robin Hood (1973)

As Robin Hood's sidekick, this big bear steals from the rich and gives to the poor. He also frequently has to help his friend Robin Hood get out of trouble. Loyal through and through, Little John sometimes worries about Robin, saying, "You know somethin', Robin? You're takin' too many chances." Still, Little John always takes those chances along with his pal, and together they make quite a team.

Little John's big question

"I was just wondering . . . are we good guys or bad guys?"

Everyone's having a swingin' good time!

Did You Know . . . ?

Phil Harris, the actor who provided the voice for Little John, also did the voice for another big animated bear—Baloo in *The Jungle Book*.

The Lost Boys

First appearance: Peter Pan *(1953)*

In Never Land, Peter Pan lives inside the hollow Hangman's Tree along with the Lost Boys, a group of boys who play treasure hunt, battle pirates, and engage in other games all day long. The Lost Boys love their fun lifestyle, but sometimes—like when Wendy visits—they realize how much they miss things such as bedtime stories. Still, when they are given the choice, they decide to stay in Never Land with their fearless leader, Peter Pan, instead of returning to London with Wendy, Michael, and John Darling.

Can you name all the Lost Boys?

- Cubby (dressed like a bear)
- Slightly, also known as Foxy (dressed in a fox suit)
- Nibs, also known as Rabbit (dressed in a rabbit suit)
- The Twins (dressed in raccoon suits)
- Tootles, also known as Skunk (dressed in a skunk suit)

The Lost Boys are off on another exciting adventure!

101

Mack

First appearance:
Disney • Pixar's Cars (2006)

Did You Know . . . ?

Mack's trailer may look like any other on the outside, but inside it's nothing but luxury—multiple TVs, a massage chair, and more!

A dedicated member of the Rust-eze Medicated Bumper Ointment team, Mack is Lightning McQueen's trusted driver. He is responsible for pulling Lightning's trailer to all his races. An experienced trucker with a lot of miles behind him, Mack knows the rules of the road, but he is willing to push his own limits to get Lightning wherever he needs to go.

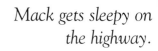

Mack gets sleepy on the highway.

The Mad Hatter

First appearance:
Alice in Wonderland (1951)

The lisping Mad Hatter, who celebrates *un*birthdays, confuses poor, lost Alice as she travels throughout Wonderland. With wild hair, two large front teeth, and a hat with the tag still attached, the Mad Hatter is goofy, silly, and full of whimsy.

Did You Know . . . ?

After dunking a watch in almost every food item on the tea table, the Mad Hatter suddenly stops, deciding that, for some reason, he should not dunk the watch in the mustard: "Mustard? Don't let's be silly!"

He's mad as a hatter!

Mad Madam Mim

First appearance:
The Sword in the Stone (1963)

The magnificent, marvelous Mad Madam Mim is an age-old nemesis of the great wizard Merlin. When Merlin challenged Mim to a wizards' duel, it was a true battle of powers between good and evil. In the duel, they could turn themselves into any true-life animal—from goats to crabs to tigers to rhinos. The important rule was that they couldn't become make-believe creatures—which Madam Mim quickly broke when she turned herself into a dragon.

Not-So-Cool Quotes

"Bat gizzards!"

"Black sorcery is my cup of tea."

"Did I say no purple dragons?"

Tricky Trivia

Q: How does Merlin finally defeat Madam Mim in the wizards' duel?

A: By turning himself into a germ and giving her a terrible, rare disease

Mim captures Wart.

Madame Medusa

First appearance: The Rescuers (1977)

Madame Medusa is one vicious villainess. She takes a little girl named Penny and her favorite teddy bear from an orphanage because Penny is small enough to enter a cave where a huge diamond is hidden. Penny doesn't like or trust the cruel "Auntie Medusa," and when she disobeys her, the wicked woman roars, "You get down there and find that big diamond or you will never see that teddy again!"

Did You Know . . . ?

During the final chase scene in *The Rescuers*, Medusa puts one foot on the back of each of her crocodiles and speeds around the swamp.

Tricky Trivia

Q: What are the names of Medusa's two crocodiles?

A: Nero and Brutus

Madame Medusa goes down!

Maggie, Grace, and Mrs. Caloway

First appearance:
Home on the Range *(2004)*

Dairy cows Maggie, Grace, and Mrs. Caloway are determined to save their idyllic little farm, Patch of Heaven. They plan on capturing the West's most notorious cattle rustler, Alameda Slim, and using the reward money to pay off their owner Pearl's debt. But nabbing Slim is no stroll through the pasture—especially when the cows' strong personalities start butting heads.

Did You Know . . . ?

• As leader of Patch of Heaven, Mrs. Caloway is a bit stuffy—and used to getting her way.
• Maggie, the newcomer to the farm, is a three-time winner of the Golden Udder Award and the original Miss Happy Heifer.
• Cheerful Grace is always optimistic and utterly tone deaf.

The cows in a runaway mine car!

Grace   Maggie   Mrs. Caloway

Maid Marian

First appearance:
Robin Hood (1973)

Even though Maid Marian is of royal birth, she is Robin Hood's one true love. Luckily for Robin, Maid Marian returns his affections, even though he steals from the likes of her in order to give to the poor. But despite the fact she is related to the greedy Prince John, she has a good heart and supports Robin Hood fully.

Tricky Trivia

Q: Who is Maid Marian?

A: She is King Richard's niece.

Q: When King Richard attends his niece's wedding to Robin Hood, what does he say?

A: "Now I have an outlaw for an in-law."

Here comes the bride—and groom!

Maleficent

First appearance:
Sleeping Beauty (1959)

Enraged because she wasn't invited to Princess Aurora's birth celebration, the dark fairy Maleficent curses the new princess: "Before the sun sets on her sixteenth birthday, she shall prick her finger on the spindle of a spinning wheel and die!" After Maleficent hears that the three good fairies—Flora, Fauna, and Merryweather—have hidden the baby in order to save her, she spends the next sixteen years of her life searching for the princess. When at last the curse is fulfilled, Maleficent's happiness is short-lived. Thanks to the good fairies and the brave Prince Phillip, the wicked sorceress is defeated, and Princess Aurora is awoken from the spell.

Not-So-Cool Quote

"You poor, simple fools, thinking you could defeat me. Me, the mistress of all evil!"

Tricky Trivia

Q: Where is Maleficent's lair?

A: The Forbidden Mountains

Q: What does Maleficent finally transform herself into in an effort to defeat Prince Phillip?

A: A fire-breathing dragon

Maleficent and Diablo

108

Marlin

First appearance:
Disney • Pixar's Finding Nemo *(2003)*

This nervous and scared clownfish suddenly turns into a hero when his only son, Nemo, is captured by a scuba diver. As soon as Nemo is scooped into the diver's bag, Marlin finds the courage he lost a long time ago. Facing sharks, a forest of jellyfish, and the whole of the wide-open sea, Marlin does not hesitate to do everything it takes to find Nemo. And when Marlin finally does find his son, no one is prouder of him than Nemo himself.

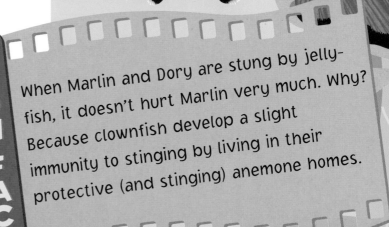

FUN FACT

When Marlin and Dory are stung by jellyfish, it doesn't hurt Marlin very much. Why? Because clownfish develop a slight immunity to stinging by living in their protective (and stinging) anemone homes.

"I would feel better if you'd go play over on the sponge beds."

Mater

First appearance:
Disney • Pixar's Cars (2006)

Mater is a good old boy with a big heart—and the only tow truck in Radiator Springs. Though a little rusty (okay, a lot), he has the quickest towrope in Carburetor County and always lends a helping hand. Mater's the first, in fact, to befriend Lightning McQueen when he rolls in to town, and he always gives the race car the benefit of the doubt.

Mater hangs out with Lightning as the race car repairs the road.

Cool Quotes

"Dad-gum it!"

"Woo-hoo! I'm happier than a tornado in a trailer park!"

"Don't need to know where I'm goin'. Just need to know where I've been."

Tricky Trivia

Q: What color was Mater originally painted?

A: Light blue

Q: Mater claims that he is the world's best what?

A: Backward driver

Q: What does Lightning promise Mater?

A: To get him a ride in a helicopter

Mater has a big heart.

Meeko and Flit

First appearance: Pocahontas (1995)

Pocahontas loves Meeko the raccoon and Flit the hummingbird, her two best non-human friends. They keep her company, and they keep her laughing. When she first sees John Smith, Pocahontas hides from him, while Flit distracts him . . . and Meeko eats his biscuits. Meeko even manages to teach Ratcliffe's spoiled pug, Percy, how to have fun in the wilds of America. At first, Meeko and Percy fight all the time. But when Percy ends up stuck in a log after one such squabble, the two actually become friends. The raccoon even manages to get Percy to dress in some Native American garb by the end of the film.

Meeko revives a waterlogged Flit.

Megara

First appearance: Hercules (1997)

When Hercules first meets the lovely Megara, he tries to save her from the river guardian Nessus. But she tells him to get lost. Still, Hercules insists on trying to save her. Meg ends up being touched by how nice the handsome Herc is. As their relationship develops, she finds herself falling in love. In the end, Hercules' true sacrifice and his willingness to give up being a god are enough to convince Meg that Hercules is the man of her dreams.

Tricky Trivia

Q: Why does Meg do whatever Hades asks of her?

A: She has sold her soul to him in order to save one of her former boyfriends. She has to do what Hades says (until Hercules rescues her from her fate).

Q: Why is Meg hesitant to fall in love with Hercules?

A: She is still recovering from having her heart broken. It is not until she gets to know Hercules that she learns that he is her one true love.

Hello, handsome!

The Mice

First appearance: Cinderella *(1950)*

Some of Cinderella's best friends are the tiny animals who live in the château along with her stepfamily. Cinderella supplies her mouse friends with clothes and food. They provide her company during her times alone in her attic room, and make her a dress for the ball. Later, they help free Cinderella from her locked room so that she can let the Grand Duke know the glass slipper belongs to her.

Tricky Trivia

Q: What are the names of Cinderella's mouse friends?

A: Jaq, Bert, Luke, Mert, Gus, Perla, and Suzy

Three kind mice

FUN FACT

The mice speak a sort of gibberish that is understandable to Cinderella . . . and to you if you listen carefully:

- "Flinderelly" means "Cinderella."
- "Attsa gud" means "That's good."
- "Roosafee" means "Lucifer."

MICKEY MOUSE

First appearance:
Steamboat Willie *(1928)*

This little guy started it all for Walt Disney when he became the star of a number of Walt's earliest cartoons. Sometimes shy, sometimes brave, and sometimes silly, Mickey is a dog's best friend (to Pluto) and an all-around nice guy. Mickey Mouse can go almost anywhere and do almost anything.

Mickey and Pluto go fishing.

In his first movie, *Steamboat Willie*, Mickey was a steamboat operator and met his girlfriend, Minnie Mouse. Later he took his sweetheart on a wild and crazy plane ride in *Plane Crazy*. Over the years, Mickey has taken on more dramatic roles, facing a giant in *Brave Little Tailor* and becoming a firefighter in *Mickey's Fire Brigade*. But no matter how serious his roles, Mickey always adds fun and laughter to all his cartoons.

FUN FACT

Here are just a few of the jobs Mickey has held: firefighter, tailor, truck driver, pilot, storekeeper, detective, sorcerer's apprentice, farmer.

Mike Wazowski

First appearance: Disney • Pixar's
Monsters, Inc. (2001)

Mike is living the good life in Monstropolis. He is in love with a beautiful, snake-haired monster named Celia, and he's the scare assistant and best friend to Sulley, the top Scarer at Monsters, Inc. But when a little human girl enters their lives, Mike and Sulley must change the way they think about everything . . . from their status at Monsters, Inc., to the very way they collect energy for the city of Monstropolis. In the end, when the monsters discover they can collect more energy from children's laughter than from their screams, Mike really comes into his own. He's much better at making kids laugh than at scaring them!

"Make it stop, Sulley! Make it stop!"

FUN FACTS

When Mike first meets human toddler Boo, he is terrified of her. Here are some of the things he says about the harmless little girl:

• "It's okay! It's all right! As long as that [Boo] doesn't come near us, we're gonna be okay."
• "That *thing* [Boo] is a killing machine!"
• "Sulley, you're not supposed to name it!"

Tricky Trivia

Q: What does Celia call Mike?
A: Googly Bear
Q: What does Mike call Celia?
A: Schmoopsie-Poo

116

Milo Thatch

First appearance: Atlantis: The Lost Empire
(2001)

Milo Thatch wants nothing more
than to pursue his late grandfather's
dream of finding the lost city of Atlantis.
Luckily, the eccentric millionaire Preston
Whitmore finds Milo and asks him to
join a fully funded expedition to discover
Atlantis. Unluckily, the people leading
the expedition are less friendly and well-
meaning than Preston Whitmore. When
the crew finally gets to Atlantis, trouble
ensues. With the aid of the Atlanteans
themselves, Milo helps to beat the bad
guys and save Atlantis. And he falls in
love in the process.

Welcome to Atlantis!

Tricky Trivia

Q: What's the name of Milo's
   grandfather?

A: Thaddeus Thatch

Q: What was Milo trained to be?

A: A cartographer and a linguist

Q: What is Milo's middle name?

A: James

MINNIE MOUSE

First appearance:
Steamboat Willie *(1928)*

Minnie Mouse is Mickey's longtime girlfriend and best buddy. Although she can be shy and quiet, she's also quite capable of beating up a few bad guys—especially if they're being mean to Mickey! Her best girl pal is Daisy Duck, and the two friends love to spend an afternoon shopping together and talking about Donald and Mickey.

True love

Did You Know . . . ?

Mickey and Minnie Mouse share the same birthday: November 18. This is the same day as the release of the first cartoon short in which they starred: Steamboat Willie.

Mowgli

First appearance: The Jungle Book (1967)

When Mowgli was just a baby, the panther Bagheera found him abandoned in a broken boat. Bagheera took the "Man-cub" to live with a family of wolves. The little boy grows up happy and carefree in the jungle . . . until the tiger Shere Khan begins to stalk him. It is then that Bagheera agrees to take the boy to a human village, where he rightfully belongs and can be protected from the wilds of the jungle. However, Mowgli doesn't want to leave the jungle, and he runs away, meeting up with a big, friendly bear named Baloo. After some wild adventures, Bagheera catches up with the pair, and Mowgli finally agrees to follow a pretty little girl into the village where he can live among humans like himself.

Who is Mowgli?

Mowgli is always trying to prove he is brave enough to stay in the jungle: "I'm not afraid. I can look after myself."

When Mowgli meets Baloo, the little guy decides he likes Baloo's life: "Yeah, man. I like being a bear."

Oops!

Mr. Incredible
(aka Bob Parr)

First appearance:
Disney • Pixar's The Incredibles *(2004)*

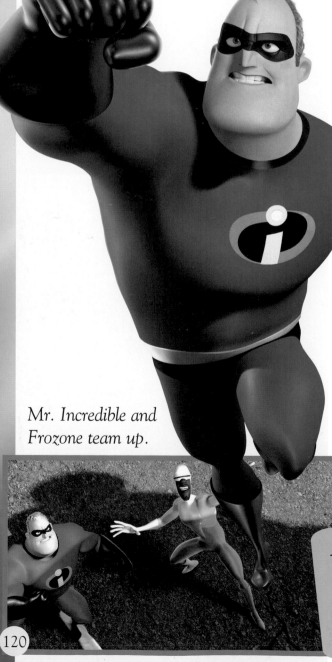

Once the best-known Super alive, Mr. Incredible finds living life full time as Bob Parr, a mild-mannered insurance adjuster under the government's Superhero Relocation Program, more than a little unfulfilling. That's why when he gets the opportunity to don his suit once more and battle a renegade robot on an uncharted island, he can't say no.

Cool Quotes

"No matter how many times you save the world, it always manages to get into jeopardy again."

"Be true to yourself."

Tricky Trivia

Q: While living undercover as Bob Parr, what does Mr. Incredible do for living?

A: He's a claim adjuster for Insuricare.

Mr. Incredible and Frozone team up.

Did You Know . . . ?

Mr. Incredible's original suit was blue.

Mrs. Potts and Chip

First appearance:
Beauty and the Beast (1991)

It's tough to be a teapot when you were once the bustling housekeeper of a castle (or a teacup, after having been a little boy). But Mrs. Potts and her son Chip make the best of it. They were transformed into enchanted objects, just like all the other castle servants, and they live in the cupboard with Chip's brothers and sisters. Mrs. Potts remains ever warm and friendly. Chip, who's got a little chip on his rim, is always energetic, fun-loving, and inquisitive.

Cool Quotes

Mrs. Potts gives Belle some good advice: "Cheer up, child. It'll turn out all right in the end. You'll see."

Chip always wants to stay up past his bedtime.

Did You Know . . . ?

Chip is the one who rescues Belle and her father after they have been locked in their cottage by Gaston's men.

Mufasa

First appearance:
The Lion King (1994)

Mufasa, the great Lion King, wants nothing more than to teach his son, Simba, how to be a good ruler. He teaches Simba about bravery, the importance of protecting those around him, and the great Circle of Life. He also tells Simba about the kings of the past . . . and how they live in the stars above, watching over those who still live on Earth. After his father's death, for which he blames himself, Simba finds that these important lessons carry him through. Later, Simba remembers his father's words when he takes over his rightful reign as king of the Pride Lands.

Cool Quotes

"A king's time as ruler rises and falls like the sun. One day, Simba, the sun will set on my time here and will rise with you as the new king."

"Being brave doesn't mean you look for trouble."

The king and queen of the Pride Lands gaze at their new son.

Mulan

First appearance: Mulan (1998)

When her frail father is summoned to fight for the Chinese army, Mulan will do anything to save him—including dressing herself as a man and joining the army in his place. But when the time comes to actually fight, she sees how difficult and dangerous her new job is. Using her quick wits, she manages to cause an avalanche that overcomes the enemy. But there's one problem: when she saves her captain, Shang, she is knocked unconscious. And when she awakens, she finds out that Shang knows she is a woman. Disgraced, Mulan is left behind by Shang and the rest of his army. But when she sees the leader of the enemy headed toward the Imperial City, she regains her courage and strength, and pursues him. In the end, she manages to save the Emperor himself . . . and bring pride and honor to her beloved family. And Shang even follows her home to thank her personally!

Tricky Trivia

Q: What does Mulan call herself when she joins the army?

A: Ping

Q: What is Mulan's family name?

A: Fa

Q: What is the name of Mulan's dog?

A: Little Brother

Mulan arrives at the army camp in disguise.

Mushu

First appearance: Mulan (1998)

This fast-talking, troublemaking little dragon follows Mulan on her adventures in the army. He does it in order to save the Fa family name and regain his status as Fa family guardian. When Mulan first meets Mushu, she is startled to see that her ancestors have sent a little "lizard" to protect her. Nevertheless, Mushu does end up helping Mulan, even becoming one of her greatest allies in the final battle against Shan-Yu.

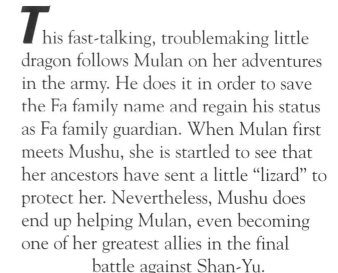

Mushu catches up on the news.

Cool Quotes

"Man, you are one lucky bug!"

"Okay, people! People! Look alive! Let's go! C'mon! Get up! Let's move it. Rise and shine. You're all way past the beauty-sleep thing. Trust me!"

FUN FACT

Mushu seems to be the only one who understands Cri-Kee's speech. He often interprets the little cricket's chirping.

Nala

First appearance:
The Lion King (1994)

As Simba's first best friend, and later his mate, Nala is faithful to the end. She loves Simba for who he is, and she believes in his worth as the true king of the Pride Lands, even after he exiles himself for years. When Simba returns to face Scar, Nala follows him and helps him claim his place as king of the Pride Lands.

Tricky Trivia

Q: What is the name of Nala's mother?

A: Sarafina

Cool Quotes

Little Nala (about Zazu): "So, how are we going to ditch the dodo?"

Adult Nala (to Simba): "What else matters? You're alive. And that means you're the king."

Lions in love

Nemo

First appearance: Disney • Pixar's
Finding Nemo (2003)

Nemo and the Tank Gang

When Nemo was still just an egg, his family was attacked by a barracuda. The entire family, with the exception of Nemo and his father, Marlin, was lost. Nemo's egg was left with a tiny dent, and when he was born, he had one smaller fin. Nemo grows up happily, although his father is a bit too cautious for Nemo's taste. When it comes time to go to school, Nemo asserts his independence. He swims out into the open sea and is captured by a scuba diver. Nemo's father begins the search of his life to find his son and bring him home. Meanwhile, Nemo is placed in a dentist's office fish tank where he meets a group of goofy new friends. In the end, Marlin finds Nemo, but before they can return home, Nemo insists on saving Marlin's friend Dory and a group of fish caught in a fishing net. When Nemo succeeds, he is truly a hero. Father and son return home, triumphant, happy, and glad to be together again.

Tricky Trivia

Q: What is the name of the "volcano" in the fish tank?

A: Mount Wannahockaloogie

Q: What was the name of Nemo's mother?

A: Coral

Oliver

First appearance:
Oliver & Company (1988)

At the beginning of *Oliver & Company*, a box of kittens is placed on a sidewalk in New York City, along with a sign reading KITTENS NEED HOME. Gradually, passersby adopt all of the kittens—except for Oliver. Oliver has to fend for himself on the streets and eventually finds a home among some outcast dogs living on a barge with their down-and-out owner, Fagin. Later, a little girl named Jenny meets Oliver and offers him a loving home. Then he must decide between living with his adoptive dog family or with Jenny. He chooses Jenny, but in order to stay with her, he must first escape from catnappers and fight off a vengeful mobster. In the end, Oliver finds a happy home—with Jenny—but his dog friends still come by to visit.

Tricky Trivia

Q: Can you name all the dogs who live with Fagin on the barge?

A: Tito (*the Chihuahua*)
Dodger (*the mutt who first finds Oliver*)
Einstein (*the Great Dane*)
Francis (*the bulldog*)
Rita (*the Afghan hound*)

Oliver and Dodger

Olivia Flaversham

First appearance:
The Great Mouse Detective (1986)

"Oh, Daddy! You made this just for me? You're the most wonderful father in the whole world!"

Sweet and stubborn, little Olivia Flaversham is lucky to have a toy-maker for a father. At the beginning of the film, Olivia receives a mechanical dancing doll from her clever dad. But soon her father is kidnapped, and Olivia turns to Basil of Baker Street and Dr. Dawson to help her find him. They search for Olivia's father in London, which has been transformed by preparations for Queen Moustoria's Diamond Jubilee. In the end, Olivia is reunited with her beloved father.

Tricky Trivia

Q: Can you name Basil's housekeeper?

A: Mrs. Judson

Q: What is the name of Ratigan's cat?

A: Felicia

Q: Where is Olivia when Dr. Dawson finds her?

A: The little mouse is crying inside a human-sized boot.

Did You Know . . . ?

England's Queen Victoria celebrated her Diamond Jubilee in 1897. She had been the ruler for sixty years. Queen Moustoria's Diamond Jubilee was to be a similar occasion . . . on a smaller scale.

O'Malley

First appearance: The Aristocats (1970)

For a fella who's really just an alley cat, Thomas O'Malley has all the charm of a full-fledged aristocat. In fact, when he rescues the lovely Duchess, along with her three kittens, he becomes their hero—and Duchess's sweetheart. With courage, street smarts, and a talent for dancing to the tunes of his jazz-jamming tomcat pals, this cat is one swell guy.

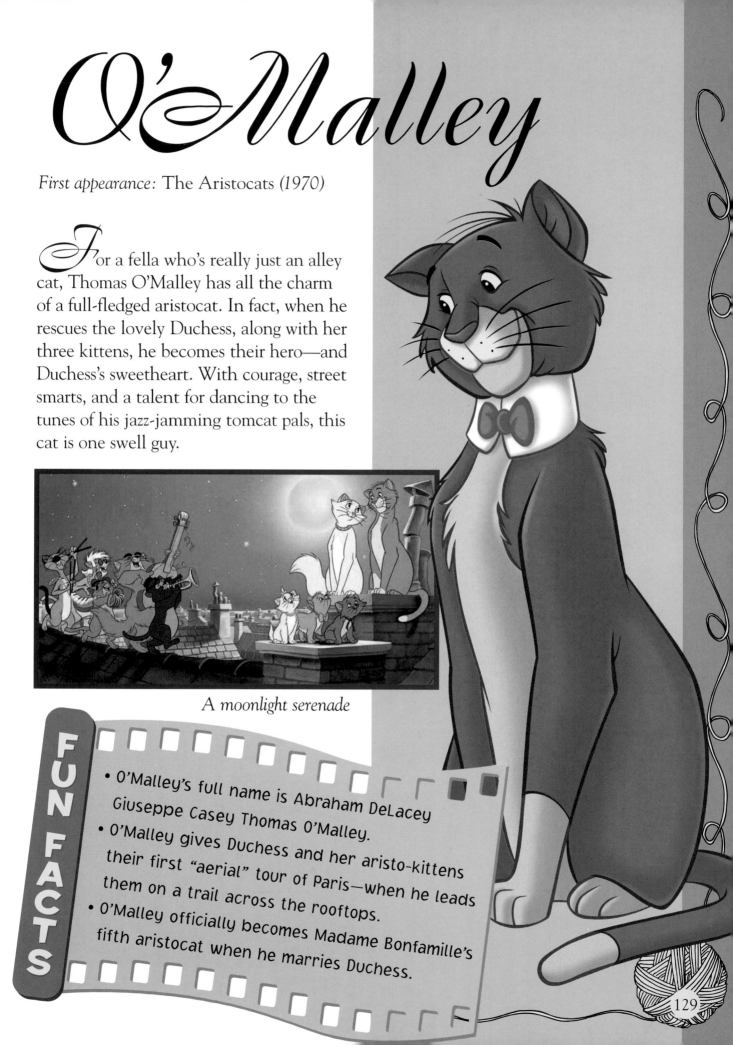

A moonlight serenade

FUN FACTS

- O'Malley's full name is Abraham DeLacey Giuseppe Casey Thomas O'Malley.
- O'Malley gives Duchess and her aristo-kittens their first "aerial" tour of Paris—when he leads them on a trail across the rooftops.
- O'Malley officially becomes Madame Bonfamille's fifth aristocat when he marries Duchess.

P.T. Flea . . .

First appearance: Disney • Pixar's
A Bug's Life (1998)

P.T. Flea is the owner of a tiny circus group made up of bugs. It's none other than P.T. Flea's World's Greatest Circus, chock-full of acts like the Chinese Cabinet of Metamorphosis, a bug-sized cannon made from a human eyedropper, and the marvelous grand finale—Flaming Death!—in which P.T. himself hurtles toward a lit match. Unfortunately, these acts often end in mishap, and after yet another disastrous performance one night, P.T. fires the entire circus gang. They go to work for an ant named Flik, who wants them to rescue his colony. But the feisty flea isn't about to give up his hopes of earning a fortune as a circus owner. So, he goes to retrieve his performing bugs and discovers they've come up with a new act—they are now warrior bugs who help save a colony of ants from a gang of greedy grasshoppers.

FUN FACT

There was another famous showman, also with the initials P.T. His name was P.T. Barnum, and he lived from 1840 to 1891. He helped to found the world-famous group now called the Ringling® Bros. and Barnum & Bailey Circus. One of his famous shows included a giant elephant named Jumbo.

and his circus gang

The circus gang's all here!

The circus gang:

Manny is the aging praying mantis who claims he was once a world-famous magician. (Yeah, right!)

Gypsy is Manny's exotically beautiful moth wife, who serves as Manny's assistant in all his magic tricks.

Heimlich is a large, very hungry caterpillar who dreams of becoming a beautiful butterfly one day. In the circus act, he plays a clown.

Tuck and Roll are Hungarian pill bugs. They are also brothers. Even though no one can really understand them, they often nod and applaud to convey their enthusiasm. In the circus act, they are acrobatic clowns.

Rosie is the black widow spider who does the high-wire act and also doubles as "tamer of the beast."

Dim is the "beast," a big rhinoceros beetle. Though Dim is large and scary, he is really a softie. Rosie treats him like a child.

Francis may be a ladybug, but he is very much a guy. Whenever he goes onstage (where he performs as a clown dressed like a flower), everyone thinks he is a female. When he becomes angry and starts yelling at the audience members, they quickly realize they have one tough little bug on their hands.

Slim the walking stick is a Shakespearean actor at heart, who has been reduced to performing as a clown dressed as a flower in P.T. Flea's circus act. But the disgruntled actor finds more excitement and glamour than he could have imagined when Flik comes to town and hires the entire circus team to defeat the grasshoppers. The melodramatic Slim actually does some real hero work defeating the bad guys, and finds the ants are more grateful than any audience.

Penny

First appearance: Bolt (2008)

Did You Know . . . ?

Penny was eight years old when she picked Bolt out at the pet store.

Penny chose Bolt from the pet shop when he was just a puppy—but he was much more the TV studio's dog than her own. She knew, of course, that she and Bolt were just actors in a TV show, but the director insisted she let Bolt believe that he was really a superdog. Penny, of course, felt terrible for him. She wished she could take Bolt home after work and show him what it was like to be a real dog . . . till one day when she had her chance.

FUN FACT

Miley Cyrus, best known for her role on the Disney Channel show *Hannah Montana*, is the voice of Penny.

Bolt and Penny in the park

132

Penny

First appearance: The Rescuers (1977)

Penny lives in an orphanage until Madame Medusa snatches her up. Why? Because Medusa needs a child small enough to enter a tiny cave where a valuable stolen diamond has been stashed. Luckily, Penny is smart and feisty . . . and has two small mouse friends named Bernard and Bianca to help her out. In the end, Penny and her pals defeat Medusa . . . and Penny (and her beloved Teddy) are adopted into a happy home.

Cool Quote

"But whoever adopts me has to adopt Teddy, too."

Tricky Trivia

Q: What are the names of the muskrats who help Bernard and Bianca rescue Penny?

A: Luke and Ellie Mae

A penny for your thoughts

Peter Pan

First appearance: Peter Pan (1953)

Peter Pan is a boy who will never, ever grow up. Luckily, he lives in Never Land, so remaining a child forever is actually possible. Peter loves living in Never Land, where he leads the Lost Boys on countless adventures, including going on treasure hunts, fighting pirates, meeting mermaids, and playing with a little fairy named Tinker Bell. He rarely ventures outside Never Land, but when he does, the real fun begins! It is one of his outside adventures that brings Wendy, Michael, and John Darling to Peter's world.

The Darling children love their time with Peter—especially when they first learn to fly. Unfortunately, Wendy has to endure some jealous pranks from Tinker Bell, but Peter takes care of things by banishing Tink for her naughty behavior. Tinker Bell soon returns, though. After all, she is one of Peter's best friends. Peter's heroics include rescuing Tiger Lily from Captain Hook and eventually battling all the pirates in order to save Wendy, Michael, John, and the Lost Boys.

Peter shows Wendy the splendors of Never Land.

Tricky Trivia

Q: How do the Darling children learn to fly?

A: With faith, trust, and a sprinkling of pixie dust from Tinker Bell

Q: If Peter Pan were to visit you, how much older would he be than when he was in the film?

A: He'd be exactly the same age. He never grows up!

Did You Know...?

Tinker Bell only jingles (and doesn't talk), but Peter understands her perfectly.

135

Phil

First appearance: Hercules (1997)

Poor Phil has tried . . . and failed . . . at training numerous heroes before he meets Hercules. At first, he is wary of the gangly teenager who comes looking for help. But then, Zeus shoots a well-placed lightning bolt at Phil in order to assure him that Hercules is indeed the son of the most powerful god on Olympus, and Phil decides to work with Hercules. Over time, Hercules goes from awkward to awesome, and Phil turns out to be one of the superhero's best friends.

A sarcastic satyr and a puzzled Pegasus

FUN FACTS

- Phil's full name is Philoctetes.
- Phil is a satyr (half goat, half man).

Did You Know . . . ?

A satyr was a creature in ancient Greek mythology that lived in the woods.

Piglet

First appearance: Winnie the Pooh and the Blustery Day *(1968)*

"**t**he little pink guy" (as Tigger sometimes calls him) is one of the most faithful friends in the Hundred-Acre Wood, even though he's sometimes forgotten because of his size (which is very small). In fact, Piglet is so small that he could be swept away by a stiff breeze, along with the leaves he might be raking from his very neat front yard. An expert at baking haycorn pie and keeping his little house tidy, Piglet is a wonderful friend. And though he finds it hard to be brave, he always seems to gather the courage to help out a friend in need.

Cool Quotes

"Oh, mercy me!"

"It's hard to be brave."

"Oh, d-d-d-dear!"

tricky trivia

Q: After a very blustery day in the Wood, to whom does Piglet give up his house?

A: Owl

Q: What is Piglet's favorite food?

A: Haycorns!

Falling leaves keep Piglet busy.

Pinocchio

First appearance: Pinocchio (1940)

After the Blue Fairy grants life to a puppet named Pinocchio, she promises to someday turn him into a real boy if he can prove himself brave, truthful, and unselfish. Unfortunately, even with the help of his conscience, Jiminy Cricket, Pinocchio finds it hard to always be good. He takes the stage at a puppet show, lies to the Blue Fairy, and ends up in big trouble at Pleasure Island. But when Pinocchio risks his own life to save his father from a terrible whale—his first truly selfless act—he finally proves that he's worthy of becoming a real boy.

Pinocchio's Nose

When the Blue Fairy asks Pinocchio why he didn't go to school, Pinocchio lies to get out of trouble. As his lie about being kidnapped grows bigger, so does his nose:

Pinocchio: They chopped me into firewood! [*Pinocchio's nose grows longer.*] Oh! Look! My nose! What's happening?

Blue Fairy: Perhaps you haven't been telling the truth, Pinocchio.

Pip

First appearance: Enchanted (2007)

Pip the chipmunk is Giselle's best friend and fiercely protective of her. Like most animals in the fairy-tale world, he has no trouble talking to humans while in Andalasia, but the minute he goes to the real world to rescue Giselle, he loses this ability completely. Though small, Pip is still big enough to keep Giselle from eating two poisoned apples and to help her escape from both a terrible troll and an evil dragon.

Cool Quotes

"I gotta lay off the nuts."
"Oh, no you don't, ya big lug!"

Tricky Trivia

Q: What is the name of the best-selling book Pip writes when he returns from New York City?

A: *Silence Isn't Golden*

Q: When Nathaniel finds Pip in an Italian restaurant, where does Pip hide?

A: Under a pizza!

Pip and Giselle notice that her prince sculpture is missing one very important feature: lips!

PLUTO

First appearance:
The Moose Hunt (1931)

Pluto is Mickey Mouse's ever-faithful favorite pup. Though he never speaks, Pluto is always very clear about his feelings. Friendly, loyal, and protective of Mickey Mouse, Pluto is also rather mischievous. He often gets into trouble, only to "apologize" by sheepishly putting his tail between his legs or bowing his head when Mickey confronts him.

COOL QUOTE

"Don't worry, Pluto. You're a better dog than any of them!"–Mickey Mouse

Did You Know . . . ?

Pluto appeared in two Mickey Mouse short films before making his first appearance under the name of Pluto. (In the first film, he had no name; in the second, he was called Rover!)

Merry Christmas, Pluto!

Pocahontas

First appearance: Pocahontas (1995)

Pocahontas loves the land where she grew up, from the waterfalls to the animals to the plants. In fact, one of her favorite advisers is Grandmother Willow, the spirit of a willow tree. When John Smith enters her life, Pocahontas discovers he shares her love of adventure and her desire to understand the unknown. Soon they find themselves falling in love with each other, despite the fact that their people are enemies. John Smith gets into trouble when trying to protect himself from a man in Pocahontas's tribe. Meanwhile, Governor Ratcliffe is trying to take over the land inhabited by Pocahontas's people, and he is willing to do anything to get his way. The brave Pocahontas throws herself in front of her own father's weapon to keep him from harming John Smith. She not only saves John Smith but also prevents both of their peoples from engaging in a war neither will ever win.

Tricky Trivia

Q: What is the name of the Indian warrior who wants to marry Pocahontas?

A: Kocoum

Pocahontas and Meeko float down the river.

Pongo and Perdita

First appearance:
101 Dalmatians (1961)

When Pongo the Dalmatian spots another lovely Dalmatian walking her human "pet," Anita, he drags *his* pet, Roger, to the park so they all can meet. It turns out the female human is just as lovely as her dog. And soon Roger is falling in love with Anita, while Pongo gets to court Perdita. Later, the Dalmatian couple share a double wedding with Roger and Anita, and Pongo and Perdita start a family that will rapidly grow to a total of 101 Dalmatians!

Tricky Trivia

Q: How many puppies do Pongo and Perdita have?

A: Perdita gives birth to fifteen puppies. Roger and Anita adopt the eighty-four others rescued from Cruella De Vil.

Q: Who narrates the film *101 Dalmatians*?

A: Pongo

One big, happy family!

Prince Charming

First appearance: Cinderella (1950)

Prince Charming has simply not met the woman of his dreams . . . until Cinderella enters the ballroom, and the two dance the night away. Unfortunately, Cinderella has a curfew (to which she strictly adheres), and when she runs away at the stroke of midnight, Prince Charming is left with nothing to remember her by . . . nothing, except of course, a single glass slipper. That proves to be enough for the Prince to find his love and marry her . . . and live happily ever after.

Did You Know . . . ?

When Cinderella falls in love with the man she is dancing with, she doesn't realize he's the Prince!

The charming
Prince
Charming

Prince Edward

First appearance: Enchanted (2007)

Prince Edward is the handsome prince of any fairy-tale maiden's dreams—and he knows it! He has dreams of his own, though, and when he meets Giselle in the forest, he vows to marry her the next day—even if it means following her to New York City, battling city buses, and defying his wicked stepmother, Queen Narissa.

Cool Quotes

"Trolls are fine to pass the time, but my heart longs to be joined in song!"

"Fear not, fair maiden. I am here."

Tricky Trivia

Q: What is the name of Prince Edward's white horse?

A: Destiny

Q: What color are Prince Edward's eyes?

A: Sparkly blue

The gallant Prince Edward rescues Giselle.

Prince Eric

First appearance:
The Little Mermaid (1989)

It's love at first sight when Ariel spots Prince Eric celebrating his birthday aboard his royal ship. But when the ship is suddenly caught in a terrible storm, Ariel saves the prince's life, and he falls in love with her. Unfortunately, after Ariel is forced to return to the sea and Eric to his home on land, Eric can remember little about Ariel except her beautiful voice. Then the wicked sea witch Ursula, out for revenge against Ariel's father, agrees to turn Ariel into a human for three days in exchange for her voice. While the human Ariel tries to get Eric to fall in love with her (without her voice), Ursula transforms herself into a woman named Vanessa. With Ariel's voice trapped in a shell around her neck, Vanessa convinces Eric that *she* is his one true love. With some help from her friends, Ariel goes out to their wedding ship. There, she is able to convince Eric that she is the one he loves. After Ursula is defeated, King Triton turns Ariel back into a human so she can marry Prince Eric.

Tricky Trivia

Q: What is the name of Eric's dog?

A: Max

Q: What present does Eric get for his birthday?

A: A statue of himself!

Ariel saves Eric's life.

Prince John

First appearance:
Robin Hood (1973)

When his brother, King Richard, leaves the country, the greedy Prince John takes over the king's royal duties—including collecting the taxes. Though Prince John wants nothing more than to sit on his false throne and get richer, Robin Hood soon arrives on the scene and puts the prince in his place. Robin Hood's mission: to steal from the rich (such as Prince John) and return money to the poor and needy. Robin Hood succeeds, and Prince John fails miserably.

Did You Know . . . ?

Prince John sucks his thumb and tugs his ear while he sleeps.

While Prince John sleeps, Robin Hood steals his gold.

Prince Phillip

First appearance: Sleeping Beauty (1959)

As a little boy, Prince Phillip attends a royal ceremony to welcome a neighboring princess into the world. His father promises his son's hand in marriage to the infant princess. Phillip and the princess grow up separately and meet one day by chance in the woods. There, they fall in love. Soon the princess falls under a wicked spell cast by the evil fairy Maleficent. All is resolved, however, after Phillip escapes imprisonment and defeats Maleficent. Then Phillip is at last able to give True Love's Kiss to his Sleeping Beauty, breaking the spell forever.

Tricky Trivia

Q: What are the two important things the good fairies give to Phillip to help him battle Maleficent?

A: The Shield of Virtue and the Sword of Truth

Q: What is the name of Prince Phillip's father?

A: King Hubert

The prince is about to awaken the sleeping beauty.

147

The Puppies

First appearance: 101 Dalmatians (1961)

The famous puppies are first kidnapped by the vicious Cruella De Vil, then rescued by their brave parents. However, they get lots of help along the way from the famous Twilight Barkers, some cows, and even the humans Roger and Anita. In the end, the wicked Cruella gets caught, and the puppies are free—to live happily ever after in their now quite large family.

A little late-night television

The puppies escape!

Tricky Trivia

Q: Who is the star of the puppies' favorite television show?

A: Thunderbolt

Q: What is the puppies' favorite brand of dog food?

A: Canine Crunchies

Q: Can you name six of the fifteen puppies?

A: Freckles, Lucky, Patch, Penny, Pepper, and Rolly

Did You Know . . . ?

In *101 Dalmatians*, the boy puppies wear red collars, and the girls wear blue collars.

Pongo and Perdy see spots!

Quasimodo

First appearance:
The Hunchback of Notre Dame (1996)

It's tough being the Hunchback of Notre Dame, but Quasimodo makes the best of it. Though he has been held prisoner in the bell tower of Notre Dame cathedral most of his life, Quasimodo finds ways to make himself happy—by building little models of the people he sees far below the bell tower, and talking to his friends, the birds and the gargoyles. When he finally gets the chance to go outside the cathedral, he encounters more than his share of trouble. Still, he also finds new friends . . . and manages to open his life to love and trust.

Tricky Trivia

Q: Who are Quasimodo's three gargoyle friends?
A: Hugo, Victor, and Laverne

Did You Know. . . ?

Victor Hugo was a French poet, novelist, and playwright who lived in the nineteenth century. He wrote the book that inspired the film. The gargoyles Victor and Hugo are undoubtedly a tribute to him.

Quasimodo and his new friends

The Queen of Hearts

First appearance:
Alice in Wonderland *(1951)*

Well . . . there is one positive part to Alice's meeting with the Queen of Hearts: it leads Alice to the end of her adventures in Wonderland and her return home at last. The Queen of Hearts is mean, vain, and spoiled, and she always seems ready to order her guards to cut off someone's head. Her tiny husband (the King) is less likely to throw temper tantrums, but this is mostly because he is scared of his wife.

The quarrelsome Queen

Queenly Quotes

"Off with her head!"

"Look up! Speak nicely! And don't twiddle your fingers!"

Radiator Springs
townsfolk

First appearance:
Disney•Pixar's Cars (2006)

The townsfolk enjoy the newly paved road

Back in the heyday of Route 66, Radiator Springs was a thriving town. But when a new interstate was built to bypass it, the town was forgotten . . . until one day when a hotshot race car named Lightning McQueen took a wrong turn and barreled in. The longer Lightning stayed, the more he got to know all the cars that still called Radiator Springs their home. Just as they changed him, he brought the townsfolk—and the town—back to life.

Meet the Locals

- Doc Hudson runs the Ornament Valley Mechanic Clinic and serves as the town judge.

- Fillmore is a hippie bus straight out of the sixties. From his psychedelic, tie-dye–covered geodesic dome, he sells his organic homebrew fuel.

- Flo runs the local diner, Flo's V8

Luigi

Guido

Doc Hudson

Lizzie

Sarge

Café, where she serves the "finest fuel in fifty states."

- Guido, an Italian forklift, is Luigi's best friend and faithful assistant.

- Lizzie sells bumper stickers, mud flaps, and other Route 66 memorabilia from the shop she opened after her late husband, Stanley, founded the town.

- Luigi is the proud owner of Luigi's Casa Della Tires, "Home of the Leaning Tower of Tires." Like his friend Guido, he's a fan of Italian racing and is obsessed with Ferraris.

- Ramone owns and operates Ramone's House of Body Art, the custom-body-and-paint shop. Since he hasn't had any customers to paint in years, he repaints himself daily.

- Red, the fire engine, is big and strong, but still shy and sensitive.

- Sally is charming, intelligent, and witty. She's the town attorney and owner of the Cozy Cone Motel. More than anyone, she wants to put Radiator Springs "back on the map!"

- Sarge, a veteran army vehicle, is patriotic to the core and runs Sarge's Surplus Hut.

- Sheriff keeps the peace in Radiator Springs. Regular checkups with Doc keep him in top condition to chase speeding roadsters . . . as do naps behind a shady billboard.

Fillmore

Red

Sally

Ramone

Flo

Sheriff

153

Remy

First appearance:
Disney·Pixar's Ratatouille (2007)

Did You Know ...?

La Ratatouille is the name of the restaurant Remy opens with Linguini and Colette.

Remy smells something cooking!

With a remarkable sense of smell and a genius for combining flavors, Remy is, without a doubt, like no other rat on Earth. He longs to be a chef like his idol, Auguste Gusteau, and not just a "poison sniffer" for his rat clan. When circumstances literally drop him into the kitchen of the great chef's restaurant, he finds himself living his dream of cooking (safely hidden from human eyes beneath his new friend Linguini's toque).

Cool Quotes

"I'm tired of taking. I want to make things. I want to add something to this world."

"If you are what you eat, I only want to eat the good stuff."

Tricky Trivia

Q: What is the name of the cookbook by Chef Gusteau that inspires Remy?

A: Anyone Can Cook

Robin Hood

First appearance: Robin Hood (1973)

Who steals from the rich and gives to the poor? Robin Hood, of course! He takes care of England—and her less fortunate citizens—when the king leaves the country in the hands of his greedy brother, Prince John. It's clear Robin's on the right side when he grabs rubies from greedy John and delivers food and toys to the poor children of the land. Maid Marian is so impressed, she falls in love with him!

Tricky Trivia

Q: What are Robin's helpers called?

A: The Merry Men

Q: How does Robin disguise himself at the archery tournament?

A: He dresses up like a stork.

Robin prepares to break in to the royal castle.

The Robinsons

First appearance:
Meet the Robinsons (2007)

The Robinsons are one wacky family!

The Robinson family may be incredibly bizarre, but they're the best family Lewis can dream of. Not only do they love and support each other, but they're free to do whatever makes them happy. Because of them, Lewis realizes how important it is to let go of the past and embrace the future. And the best part is they'll actually be Lewis's family one day!

Tricky Trivia

Q: How do the Robinsons toast each other?

A: By splashing water on their heads

Q: Why does the Robinsons' dog wear glasses?

A: Because his insurance won't pay for contacts

Q: How are Uncle Spike and Uncle Dmitri related?

A: No one is sure

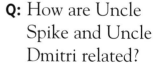

Russell and Carl Fredricksen

First appearance: Disney • Pixar's Up (2009)

Carl Fredricksen once dreamed of being an adventurer and traveling all around the world. But at age seventy-eight, he had started to feel as if life had passed him by. Carl still had one dream, however: to fly his house to the Most Beautiful Place on Earth, Paradise Falls, in honor of his late wife, Ellie.

Nine-year-old Russell, on the other hand, already considered himself an adventurer, but just needed one more badge to become an official Senior Wilderness Explorer. Then, one day, he came knocking on Carl's door—just as the house lifted off the ground and into the sky. Together . . . their adventure into the wilderness began.

Tricky Trivia

Q: As a child, Carl dreamed he'd grow up to be an explorer. But what did he really become?

A: A balloon salesman

How about some air traffic control?

Samson

First appearance: The Wild (2006)

On the loose in New York

Samson is the top lion at the New York Zoo. Everyone admires him, but no one more than his cub, Ryan, who has grown up hearing Samson's hair-raising tales of adventure in the wild. Ryan wants to be just like Samson—but it's only after the cub is accidentally shipped to Africa and Samson goes to rescue his son that Samson finally admits that he's actually captive-born. He never lived in the wild, and he couldn't survive there if he wanted to! Still, Samson proves that he's just as brave and proud as any lion from "the wild" could hope to be.

Cool Quotes . . . Samson Speaking to Himself

"Dig deep, Samson. You're a lion. Be a lion."

"You can do this. Use your instincts."

Tricky Trivia

Q: According to Samson, where does a lion find his roar?

A: In his heart

Q: Where was Samson actually born?

A: In the circus

Scar

First appearance:
The Lion King (1994)

It's bad news for Scar when Simba is born. Simba is the son and rightful heir to the Lion King, Mufasa, displacing his Uncle Scar from his right to the throne. However, it doesn't take Scar long to put an evil plan into place— by luring Simba into a thundering stampede. When Mufasa finds out Simba is in danger, he leaps to his son's rescue. Mufasa dies, and Simba feels terribly sad and guilty. Scar encourages him to run away. Unfortunately for Scar, however, Simba is the one and only true Lion King. And when he returns to take over his rightful role, the evil Scar meets his end at last.

The evil, ambitious Scar plots and schemes.

Cruel Quotes

"Well, I was first in line until that little hair ball was born."

"Run away, Simba! Run! Run away and never return!"

Tricky Trivia

Q: What are the names of the three hyenas who help Scar?

A: Shenzi, Banzai, and Ed

Q: What does Scar say he'll be when Simba becomes king?

A: A monkey's uncle

Scuttle

First appearance:
The Little Mermaid *(1989)*

Wise? Well, Scuttle the seagull has his own special way of thinking about things. Ariel and the others see him as a sort of expert on human items, but it's pretty clear he isn't very knowledgeable at all. Upon seeing a human pipe, he labels it a "snarfblatt" and says: "The snarfblatt dates back to prehysterical times when humans used to sit around and stare at each other all day. Got very boring. So they invented this snarfblatt to make fine music."

Scuttle may not be wise, but he certainly is creative!

Translations for Scuttle's Silly Words

Dinglehopper = fork
Snarfblatt = pipe
Intrepidacious = very brave
Prehysterical = prehistorical

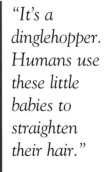

"It's a dinglehopper. Humans use these little babies to straighten their hair."

Sebastian

First appearance:
The Little Mermaid (1989)

Sebastian is the court composer for King Triton's undersea kingdom. As such, the crab is also the Little Mermaid's singing coach. When Ariel gets into trouble with her father, the blustery King Triton assigns Sebastian the task of looking after the Little Mermaid and keeping her out of trouble. Sebastian fails miserably in his quest to keep Ariel from danger (and humans), and he worries about it the whole time, often talking about how much trouble he'll be in when King Triton finds out about Ariel's antics.

Tricky Trivia
Q: What is Sebastian's full name?
A: Horatio Felonious Ignacious Crustaceous Sebastian

Sebastian's Silly Sayings
"Jumping jellyfish!"

"Somebody's got to nail that girl's fins to the floor!"

"Will you get your head out of the clouds and back in the water where it belongs?"

The King and the court composer

The Seven Dwarfs

First appearance: Snow White and
the Seven Dwarfs *(1937)*

Doc is the leader of the Seven
Dwarfs (at least in his own mind).
With glasses and a bumbling
manner of speech, he stands out
from the rest. Doc often mixes up
his words: "C'mon, hen! Eh, c'mon, men!"
"The lit's light! Eh, the light's lit!"

Grumpy is, well, usually quite
grumpy. But sometimes (like
when Snow White kisses him on
the forehead), you can catch a
glimmer of a smile on Grumpy's face.

Dopey never speaks, but he does have a
voice. (He screams when he is sent
upstairs to find out who is
sleeping in the Dwarfs' beds and
sees only a yawning figure under
a white sheet.) He also has
endearingly large ears and a wide
grin. Some would say Dopey is
actually rather smart: he's the one
who manages to dance with
Snow White by climbing
atop Sneezy's shoulders.

Sleepy (*yawn!*) has a
very difficult time
staying awake.

Seven delighted Dwarfs and one pretty princess

Happy is, well, happy. But like the other Dwarfs, he is astounded when Snow White asks them to wash up for supper. Also, he races quite seriously to the princess's rescue when the wicked Queen is giving her the poisoned apple.

Sneezy suffers from a hopeless case of hay fever . . . and anything else that can possibly make a fellow sneeze. His fellow Dwarfs are constantly looking for ways to tie up his nose in order to put off (temporarily, at least) his fits of "*Achoo!*"

Bashful, as Walt Disney once said, is secretly in love with Snow White. Of course, this makes his blushing even worse than normal, especially when she kisses him good-bye on the forehead as he sets off for work.

Tricky Trivia

Q: How many nights does Snow White spend at the Seven Dwarfs' cottage?

A. Only one!

Q: What do the Seven Dwarfs mine?

A: Diamonds

Shere Khan

First appearance:
The Jungle Book (1967)

Of all the characters in *The Jungle Book*, Shere Khan is by far the most vicious. There is not a good bone in Shere Khan's body—all he wants to do is hunt down Mowgli. Luckily, Mowgli is able to outwit the tiger. Then, along with some help from his friends, Mowgli escapes to the Man-village where he is able to live in safety. Still, Shere Khan maintains his grudge against Mowgli, so the boy will always have to be on his toes when he returns to the jungle.

Tricky Trivia

Q: How does Mowgli outwit Shere Khan?

A: Mowgli ties a fiery branch to the tiger's tail.

Q: How does Mowgli outsmart Shere Khan a second time in *The Jungle Book 2*?

A: He traps him in the mouth of a giant statue of a tiger's head.

The cruel cat grabs the slithery snake.

Silver

First appearance: Treasure Planet (2002)

John Silver, the cyborg cook on board the *Legacy*, is perhaps the most interesting character that young Jim Hawkins meets on his search for treasure. John Silver becomes Jim's friend, mentor . . . and greatest enemy. In the end, however, the cyborg pirate gives up his lifelong dream for treasure in order to save Jim. The crusty cyborg pirate proves he has a heart, after all.

Crusty Quotes

"You got the makin's of greatness in ya! But you gotta take the helm and chart your own course!"

"That treasure is owed me, by thunder!"

Did You Know . . . ?

A cyborg (pronounced "SIGH-borg") is a fictional creature that is half man, half machine. Some of the cyborgs in the *Treasure Planet* universe have mechanical arms with built-in knives, scissors, magnifying glasses, and other tools useful for active space travelers.

Jim and John Silver

Simba

First appearance:
The Lion King (1994)

Spoiled as a cub, Simba grows up living the life of a carefree prince. He believes he deserves to get whatever he wants because he is the future Lion King. But when his father is tragically killed, Simba thinks the death is his fault. Sad and torn with guilt, he runs away from his destiny. He grows up in a desert oasis with his friends, Timon and Pumbaa, ignoring his role as the king of the Pride Lands. Later, when the Pride Lands are in ruins and the animals are starving, Simba's childhood friend Nala finds him. She encourages him to return home to help the animals in the Pride Lands by becoming a good ruler. Finally, Simba gains the courage he needs when he sees his father's image in the stars above. He realizes it is time to return home, where he battles his evil Uncle Scar and takes his rightful place as the Lion King at last.

Did You Know . . . ?

• Timon is a meerkat.
• Pumbaa is a warthog.
• Rafiki is a baboon.

Zazu scolds Simba.

Tricky Trivia

Q: What are the names of Simba's parents?

A: His father is Mufasa. His mother is Sarabi.

Q: Who tells Mufasa that Simba is in trouble during the wildebeest stampede?

A: Zazu

FUN FACTS

- When Simba returns as the Lion King, Nala becomes the queen of the Pride Lands.
- In *The Lion King II: Simba's Pride*, Simba and Nala have a daughter named Kiara.

"You're Mufasa's boy."

Snow White

First appearance:
Snow White and the Seven Dwarfs
(1937)

A kiss for Dopey

Though she is royal by birth, Snow White is forced into a role of servitude as the wicked Queen's scullery maid. She dreams, however, of finding her one true love. The Prince actually does meet her at her wishing well as she is fetching water, but it is not until the end of the film that she gets her first kiss from him—the kiss of true love. That kiss, of course, breaks the evil spell put upon Snow White by the vain Queen.

Snow White's sweet and gentle nature makes her beloved by all, and even when she lives a lonely life of servitude in the Queen's castle, she is befriended by the doves that flock around her as she scrubs the stone steps.

"Oh, it's adorable. Just like a doll's house."

FUN FACT

Snow White and the Seven Dwarfs was the first full-length animated feature created by Disney.

Did You Know . . . ?

Workers at the Disney Studios applied blush to Snow White's cheeks in every single animated frame in which she appeared, just the way makeup would be applied to a real person.

Tricky Trivia

Q: How does Snow White first let the Prince know that she likes him?

A: Standing on her balcony, she kisses a dove that flies down and kisses the Prince.

Party time!

stitch

Formerly known as alien Experiment 626, Stitch accidentally ends up on Earth when he tries to escape being sent to a distant asteroid prison. He lands in Hawaii, where he is mistaken for a dog, adopted by a little girl named Lilo, and given a new name and a new life. There, he learns all about *'ohana* ("family") and gradually progresses from being a naughty alien bent on destruction to being a caring member of Lilo's family. When Lilo draws a picture of Stitch and points out his "badness level," she remarks that it is unusually high for someone his size. Lilo's right, but she doesn't even know half of what Stitch has done wrong. Here's a list of some of the naughty things Stitch does:

- He says "meega na la queesta" (the naughtiest words in the universe) to the Grand Councilwoman.
- He bites Gantu.
- He steals a police cruiser—the red one!
- He crash-lands on Earth, making a big hole and a huge mess.

"His name is . . . Stitch."

- He frightens all the pets at the animal shelter.
- He wags his rear end at Jumba and Pleakley (which, as we all know, is rather rude).
- He picks his nose.
- He steals Myrtle's trike.
- He burps.
- He takes things from the refrigerator without asking.
- He ruins pillows.
- He almost swallows Pleakley's head.
- He eats Lilo's cake and then spits it out when he decides he doesn't like it.
- He breaks things—a lot of things.

TRICKY TRIVIA

Q: Who created Stitch?

A: Jumba Jukiba

Q: Why doesn't Stitch like water when he first lands on Earth?

A: It is one of the few things that can destroy him (because he sinks in water).

TRANSLATIONS

"Noogy bay!" (an exclamation of frustration)

"Ih." (yes)

"Meega na la queesta!" (No one on Earth is quite sure what this means, but it's so bad, it makes an alien throw up!)

Sulley

First appearance:
Disney·Pixar's Monsters, Inc. (2001)

Sulley may look like a friendly, furry blue guy covered in purple spots, but if he popped out of your closet in the middle of the night, he'd look downright scary! In fact, Sulley was named top Scarer at Monsters, Inc. for a full thirty-six months in a row. Then, a little girl named Boo escaped into Monstropolis and changed his life forever. Now, Sulley collects laughs instead of screams!

Tricky Trivia

Q: When did Sulley meet his best friend, Mike?

A: In elementary school

Q: What is Sulley's full name?

A: James P. Sullivan

Q: How does Mike make it possible for Sulley to visit Boo again?

A: He rebuilds her entire closed door out of its shredded pieces.

"Mikey, there's a scream shortage. We're walking."

Terence

First appearance: Tinker Bell (2008)

Terence, a dust-keeper fairy, has a bit of a crush on Tinker Bell—ever since he first poured pixie dust over her when she arrived in Never Land. His every-day duties include doling out daily doses of pixie dust to his fellow fairies. Terence doesn't consider his job too important, until Tink convinces him that it's quite the opposite—he keeps all the magic alive!

Terence and Tink

FUN FACT

Never Land fairies receive exactly one level teacupful of fairy dust per day and not a speck more or less.

Thumper

First appearance: Bambi (1942)

One of Bambi's first and best friends, Thumper is a curious, exuberant, and sometimes overly talkative bunny. He's the one who shows the young prince around the forest when Bambi is just a few hours old, and continues to be his constant companion.

Cool Quotes

"I'm thumpin'! That's why they call me Thumper!"

When Bambi is first born, it's Thumper who spreads the news: "The new prince is born!"

Later, Thumper comments on Bambi's first steps: "Look! He's trying to get up! Kinda wobbly, isn't he?"

Thumper thumps for Bambi and Flower.

tigger

First appearance: Winnie the Pooh and the Blustery Day *(1968)*

"Hoo-hoo-hoo! Bouncin's what tiggers do best!" Well, actually, flying kites, playing Pooh Sticks, planting seeds, building houses, having parties, eating cake, and a number of other things are also what tiggers do best (at least according to Tigger, that is). Tigger is very proud of himself, and his unique status of being the onliest tigger. He is Roo's best friend and hero, and together the two have a jolly time bouncing and playing throughout the Hundred-Acre Wood, despite Rabbit's frequent angry protests.

tigger talk

Tigger often mixes up familiar sayings:

"A watched pot never spoils!"

"Goes together like oil and spinach!"

"Look both ways before bossing!"

"A friend in need is a friend who needs ya."

"Took the wind right outta my whales!"

tigger's Nicknames for his Pals

"Mrs. Kanga" (especially when he's feeling shy), "Pooh Boy," "Roo Boy," "Piglet Ol' Pal," "Beak Lips" (Owl), "Long Ears" (Rabbit), "Donkey Boy" (Eeyore)

Tigger just loves to bounce!

Timon & Pumbaa

First appearance: The Lion King (1994)

"**H**i, there. I'm Timon, and this is . . ."

"Hi."

"Tell them who you are."

"A warthog?"

"Pumbaa! Your name is Pumbaa!"

"I knew that."

"We're Timon and Pumbaa. We rescued Simba. That's right. If it weren't for us, Simba would be a goner. Kaput. Old news. We rescued him from the desert and brought him to our little home. Taught him to eat bugs. Yeah, he learned to eat bugs instead of eating us. We also taught him to stop worrying about things you don't need to worry about (also known as hakuna matata). Gee, we really are terrific, aren't we?"

Timon and Pumbaa not only saved Simba's life, they also taught him to be happy again. During the time he spent with the meerkat and warthog, Simba grew from a cub to a full-grown lion. And when the time came for him to return to the Pride Lands and claim his rightful place as king, Simba was ready, thanks to his two pals.

Cool Quotes

Timon: Gee, he looks blue.

Pumbaa: I'd say brownish gold.

Pumbaa's got himself in a tight spot!

TIMOTHY MOUSE

First appearance: Dumbo (1941)

Who says elephantsare afraid of mice? Timothy Mouse becomes Dumbo's best pal, helping the baby elephant through the tough times that follow his separation from his mother. And when Dumbo learns to fly, it's Timothy who, at the last minute, gives Dumbo the confidence he needs to realize he can fly on his own—without the help of the "magic feather."

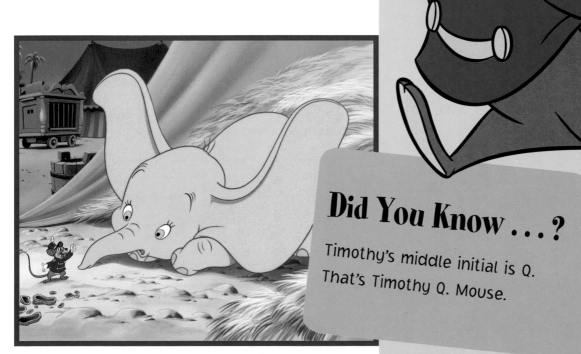

Did You Know ...?

Timothy's middle initial is Q. That's Timothy Q. Mouse.

"Look, Dumbo—I'm your friend!"

Tinker Bell

First appearance: Peter Pan (1953)

Feisty, spunky Tinker Bell is the tinker fairy who traveled with Peter Pan and the Lost Boys. But way, way before she ever met Peter Pan, Tink was born from a baby's laugh and traveled to Pixie Hollow (a hidden nook in Never Land and home to all fairies). There, she became a full-fledged fairy. At first, she wasn't pleased to find out that her talent was tinkering. She longed for something that she felt was more important. Fortunately, her fairy friends helped her realize how very special her tinker talent was.

Tink watches the light fairies make a rainbow.

Tricky Trivia

Q: Where does Tink get the idea for the pompoms on her shoes?

A: From the ballerina statue in the music box that she finds washed up on Never Land's shore

Cool Quote

"I'm a tinker. And tinkers fix things."

FUN FACT

Tinker Bell actually met Wendy Darling years before Peter Pan. When Wendy was a very young girl, Tinker Bell came to the mainland (that's the human world) and returned the child's lost music box to her.

Tod

First appearance:
The Fox and the Hound *(1981)*

When he is adopted by the loving
Widow Tweed, Tod the fox soon
becomes best friends with the young
hound Copper, who lives nearby.
However, the two are raised to be
enemies, and eventually Copper is
sent to hunt down Tod. But Copper
stays true to their childhood friendship
by defending the fox, and Tod does his
part by saving Copper from a bear. In
the end, despite all that stood between
them, the fox and hound remain fast
friends.

Tricky Trivia

Q: Who becomes Tod's girlfriend?
A: Vixey the fox

Cool Quotes

Tod: I'm a fox. My
name's Tod. What's your
name, kid?

Copper: Mine's Copper.
I'm a hound dog.

Tod: Gee, I bet you'd be
good at playing hide-
and-seek. You
wanna try, Copper?

*Tod tells Copper to
count while he hides.*

Tony

First appearance:
Lady and the Tramp *(1955)*

Who is the most romantic restaurant owner in the world? Tony, of course! When Tramp brings Lady to Tony's back alley for a meal, Tony goes all out for him, providing spaghetti for two and some romantic music, too! Why does Tony do it? He seems to know that Lady is the right gal for his favorite pooch, Tramp.

FUN FACTS

- The dinner at Tony's restaurant is Lady and Tramp's first date.
- Tony's nickname for Tramp is Butch.

Compliments of the chef!

Ursula

First appearance: The Little Mermaid (1989)

Ursula the sea witch had vowed to get revenge on Ariel's father, King Triton, ever since he banished her from the kingdom of Atlantica. So when she discovered that Ariel had fallen in love with a human prince named Eric, she quickly seized her chance. She made a deal with the mermaid to make Ariel human for three days, in exchange for the mermaid's voice. If Ariel received a Kiss of True Love by then, she could be a human forever. If not, she would join the other poor merpeople who'd lost their souls in Ursula's "garden."

Tricky Trivia

Q: What are the names of Ursula's eel henchmen?

A: Flotsam and Jetsam

Q: What does Ursula keep Ariel's voice in?

A: Her shell necklace

Not-So-Cool Quote

"It's time Ursula took matters into her own tentacles!"

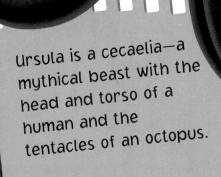

FUN FACT

Ursula is a cecaelia—a mythical beast with the head and torso of a human and the tentacles of an octopus.

WALL·E

First appearance:
Disney·Pixar's WALL·E (2008)

Did You Know . . . ?

• WALL·E stands for Waste Allocation Load Lifter Earth-class.
• WALL·E likes to collect human objects, including lightbulbs, toys, an eggbeater, and many other curious things!

WALL·E is programmed to clean up the hopelessly polluted planet Earth, one trash cube at a time. However, after 700 years, he's the only working robot left on Earth, and he's developed quite a personality. He's extremely curious and a little lonely—and it's really no surprise that when the lovely robot named EVE appears, WALL·E instantly falls in love. But he never could have imagined how big an adventure they would have together.

Tricky Trivia

Q: What is WALL·E's favorite movie?

A: *Hello, Dolly!*

Q: Before EVE landed on Earth, who was WALL·E's only friend?

A: A cockroach

WALL·E is crazy about EVE.

Wendy, John & Michael Darling

First appearance: Peter Pan (1953)

Even before they actually travel to Never Land, Wendy, Michael, and John Darling know all about Peter Pan. That's because of the stories they have been told about him. When Peter actually does enter their bedroom one night in search of his lost shadow, the three children readily agree to return with him to Never Land for a true adventure. And so, with a sprinkling of magic pixie dust from Tinker Bell (along with a good dose of faith and trust), Wendy, Michael, and John are soon able to fly . . . all the way to Never Land.

Wendy

- The oldest of the Darling children
- The subject of Tinker Bell's jealousy
- Walks the plank on Captain Hook's ship, only to be saved by Peter Pan

John

- Wears glasses and a top hat
- Carries an umbrella
- Loves playing adventure games with the Lost Boys

Michael

- The youngest of the Darling children
- Carries his teddy bear with him wherever he goes

The Darling children learn to fly.

The White Rabbit

First appearance:
Alice in Wonderland (1951)

He's late. He's very, very late. In fact, he always seems to be late. That's the White Rabbit. When he first runs past Alice with his giant watch, he declares that he is quite tardy. Curious, Alice follows him all the way to Wonderland, where her adventures begin. In fact, if it weren't for the White Rabbit, Alice would never have made it to Wonderland.

"I'm late! I'm late!"

The Wicked Queen

First appearance:
Snow White and the Seven Dwarfs (1937)

"*M*agic Mirror on the wall.
Who is the fairest one of all?"

The vain Queen consults her Magic
Mirror regularly to assure herself that she
is the most beautiful in the land. One day,
when the Magic Mirror honestly answers
that the young maiden Snow White is
fast becoming more beautiful, the wicked
Queen decides to get rid of her. Luckily,
Snow White is able to escape to the
cottage of the Seven Dwarfs. The Queen
finds the princess there, and uses her
magic powers to transform herself into an
old peddler woman and trick Snow White
into eating a poisoned apple. But even
the disguise and the magic are not
enough to keep Snow White from her
true love. The Queen finally meets
a bad end: when the Seven Dwarfs chase
her to the top of a mountain, lightning
strikes the rock she is on, and she
tumbles down, never to be seen again.

Tricky Trivia

Q: What is the one mistake
the Queen makes when
she creates the poisoned
apple?

A: The spell may be broken
by Love's First Kiss.

*"This is no ordinary apple.
It's a magic wishing apple."*

Winnie the

First appearance: Winnie the Pooh and the Honey Tree (1966)

this much beloved bear of very little brain seems always to be in search of honey. He adores his smackerels of the sticky yellow stuff, and will do just about anything to have some, including getting stuck in beehives, putting himself in danger of being stung, and overstuffing himself! Pooh's best friend is Christopher Robin, but he's also quite close to his little pal Piglet, as well as everybody else in the Hundred-Acre Wood. In fact, everybody seems to love Pooh.

Interview

Q: I say, Winnie the Pooh, it's a pleasure to have a chance to talk to you.

A: Oh, thank you. It's a pleasure that you

HUNNY

Pooh

serve such large smackerels of honey to your guests.

Q: How did you come to live in the Hundred-Acre Wood?

A: Um, I don't know.

Q: Do you like it here?

A: Oh, yes. There are lots of honeybee trees. Oh, and I have wonderful friends, too.

Q: Would you ever move?

A: Move where? To that seat over there?

Q: No, no, Pooh Bear. Would you ever move outside the Hundred-Acre Wood?

A day in the Hundred-Acre Wood with Owl, Rabbit, Piglet, Pooh, and Roo

A: Oh, I don't know. I've never been outside the Hundred-Acre Wood. I suppose I could move out there just as well as I can here. Although, I must say, I didn't think there *was* an outside!

FUN FACTS

- Pooh once ate so much of Rabbit's honey that he couldn't get out of his friend's house.
- Another time, Pooh rolled in mud and floated up to a beehive on a balloon, trying to trick the bees into thinking he was a little black rain cloud.

WOODY

First appearance: Disney•Pixar's Toy Story (1995)

Woody is at the top of the toy chain in Andy's room—until Andy gets a Buzz Lightyear toy for his birthday. With Buzz's arrival, Woody's status as favorite toy is threatened—and his role as leader of the toys is also placed in jeopardy. Soon, however, Woody learns to overcome his jealousy in favor of friendship, and he risks everything to save Buzz from Andy's toy-destroying neighbor, Sid. Later, in *Toy Story 2*, Buzz returns the favor by saving his toynapped pal from the scheming toy collector Al McWhiggin.

FUN FACTS

- Woody has a holster, but no gun.
- When Woody is toynapped in *Toy Story 2*, the toy cleaner paints over Andy's name on the bottom of Woody's boot. Later, Woody peels the paint off when he realizes his true home is with Andy.

"It's time for *Woody's Roundup*!"

TRICKY TRIVIA

Q: At the end of *Toy Story*, Woody gets a burn mark on what part of his body?

A: His forehead

Q: Under which of Woody's boots has Andy written his name?

A: The right boot

Q: What is Woody's role in *Woody's Roundup*?

A: Sheriff!

Q: Who is Woody's sweetheart?

A: Bo Peep

Q: When Woody rescues Jessie, what does he use as a lasso?

A: His pull string

COOL QUOTE

"It doesn't matter how much we're played with. What matters is that we're here for Andy when he needs us!"

EVEN COOLER QUOTE

"Look at you! You're a Buzz Lightyear! Any toy would give up his moving parts to be you. You have wings! You glow in the dark! You talk! Your helmet does that *whoosh* thing. You are a cool toy!"

YZMA

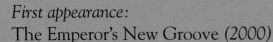

First appearance:
The Emperor's New Groove (2000)

At first, it's hard to tell who is worse: the selfish Emperor Kuzco, or his assistant Yzma who turns Kuzco into a llama and then takes over the throne. Well, they're both pretty nasty, but at least Kuzco learns his lesson. Yzma doesn't.

Here's an example of how Yzma acts:

Yzma: It's no concern of mine whether your family has—what was it again?

Peasant: Um, food.

Yzma: Ha! You really should have thought of that before you became peasants!

Yzma and Kronk choose a potion for Kuzco.

FUN FACT

Here's how Kuzco becomes a llama: Yzma asks Kronk to poison Kuzco, but the potions get mixed up, and Kuzco turns into a llama instead.

Zazu

First appearance:
The Lion King (1994)

Zazu is Mufasa's nervous adviser. He does everything from reporting on the news in the Pride Lands to babysitting Simba and Nala. Later, when Scar becomes king, Zazu continues as royal adviser, but he has to do so from his cagelike prison next to Scar. He is loyal, witty, and faithful to the end. Nobody is happier than Zazu when Simba returns to take his place as rightful king of the Pride Lands.

Zazu watches over Simba and Nala.

FUN FACTS

- Zazu is a hornbill bird.
- Zazu gives Mufasa his daily "morning report" to update the Lion King on recent news in the Pride Lands.
- Zazu sometimes acts as a babysitter to Simba . . . which neither one of them likes.

List of Characters